HOLE IN ONE

GEORGE ONSTOT

ISBN: 09881571-9-5
ISBN-13: 978-0-9881571-9-4

For T.W.

CONTENTS

PART 1:

CUTE BABES AND FEELIN' GOOD

HOLE IN ONE

1

At the conclusion of my first day, as I walked off the course, one of the reporters, a blonde cutie in a blue suit approached me for an interview. I asked Ms. Cutie to marry me, and she didn't seem to know if I was joking or not, and neither did I. After all, I, now on my third marriage, had impressed my friends with my willingness to marry people.

In the press tent, I apologized to the reporters for my tardiness, especially since I was one of the tournament leaders. But Ms. Cutie had enticed me into the press tent, sat down with me and crossed her legs. Then she told me most of what she had learned about golf, which was more than I would have guessed.

"You know more about this shit than I do," I told her, and everyone laughed. "So, how about it? Do you want to marry me?"

Everyone laughed some more, and she blushed the deepest red. Humor always worked well there, as it did everywhere else. Alas, *someone* had to be the butt of my jokes, and in this case, Ms. Cutie, a woman in a man's press tent, became the obvious victim.

"How did you like my work with the one-iron out there?" I asked her. "It poked a nice little hole out of the wind and the ball went into that cup, just like it's supposed to do."

On that last fairway, I used the right club and made the right shot. I ended up one under par, and that's about the best a person can do on a fairway that's mainly just a vast expanse of unforgiving distance.

If you don't follow golf, let me explain something: a good one-iron shot is as difficult to find in this world as a good friend. Also, a birdie on the 18th hole at Placid Oaks is something a person doesn't mind bragging about—especially when that golfer is playing at the Canadian Open, the biggest tournament in the Great White North.

I said in the press tent, "I did some things right

out there today. I put the club on the ball and let that thing sail through the air and land where Daddy said. It was like, 'School's out—time to throw away the textbooks and piss on the teacher.'"

If you haven't figured it out by now, I should explain that I am a professional golfer. That's mostly I do with my days and nights: go from one tournament to the next, playing golf.

I do this for a living because I can play well enough to be a member of the Professional Golfers Association of Canada. The PGA has a number of tournaments every year in Canada and the States, in which lots of guys like me compete for millions of dollars in prize money.

We travel and travel, here and there, more or less nonstop, like a bunch of drifters or nomads. Except we dress well and smell good. We go to Honolulu, New Orleans, Las Vegas, Pebble Beach and throughout Canada. Some of these places, of course, are glamorous; many others are not.

After a time, I've started to think that my last name was Hilton, because I've stayed at most of their hotels. I've also stayed at many Hyatts, Ramadas and

Doubletrees.

My life is for those who are OK with driving on freeways, living in hotel rooms and eating in restaurants. That's the hard part. The easy part is playing a game for my bed and board, and having fun more often than not. I have met very few PGA guys who have ever had to *work* for a living.

Also, I don't have to *win* any of those tournaments to make enough money to live comfortably. I just need to finish 24th or better each time out to keep enough cash in my pockets to drive a fancy car and wear quality clothing.

I am Teddy Crossley, mid-30s, Caucasian Canadian. Compared to Tiger Woods, I'm Teddy Nobody. But on these tournaments, I can make several hundred thousand dollars per year just by playing enough decent rounds of golf.

Frankly, I have to believe that even the most ardent sports fan loses interest in so many of these PGA tournaments, especially when the fans have 257 channels at home, and half of them feature big black guys beating up on each other or a bunch of Europeans getting killed in a spectacular, fiery auto race collision.

Once each season, the golfing gets special when major tournaments happen: the Masters, the British Open, the Canadian Open and what have you. A very serious professional golfer would trade his family and left testicle to win one of the really big events. To win any of those major buggers can make a pro's entire career worthwhile. As a Canuck, I've always been especially eager to win the Canadian Open, and I know that many of the Canadian sports reporters are secretly—or maybe openly—hoping I'll do it one day.

The thrill of winning a big one, naturally, is a big part of what drives us, pardon the pun, but it's also the chance to do endorsements and other things that bring in the megabucks. Do you think Tiger Woods got so rich just by winning all those purses?

Really, just to be way up there on the leader board can be an exhilarating experience. That's what happened to me at Placid Oaks. It got me more attention, admiration and whatnot than I could ever remember having. The Canadian sponsors also took a bit of interest in me for a little while.

Professional golf as a lucrative form of

entertainment probably started with Arnold Palmer and has continued until today. Personally, though, I think of it in terms of Before Tiger and After Tiger. Tiger Woods came along when the sport really needed him. A tall, handsome black man who excelled at golf before he was old enough to jerk off, Tiger, at age 21, started beating the hell out of every PGA guy unlucky enough to be his opponent. Soon, even people totally indifferent to sports started saying, "Who is this guy called Tiger, and why is everyone talking about him? I've got to check him out." So, they watched Tiger play golf, and in so doing, at least learned enough about the sport to figure out what made him so great.

Remember Wayne Gretzky? Folks who didn't give a rat's ass about the NHL paid attention to *him*. Thus, the Great One transcended hockey and became a cultural icon. Hockey, certainly at the NHL level, is a dangerous, fast-paced, fascinating sport, with all those big guys on ice skates, chasing the puck all over the ice and knocking each other on his ass, and sometimes nearly killing one another. Who can resist that?

I don't know if the National Football League has needed so many superstars to captivate the public. Huge guys tackling, and occasionally crippling each other over control of that pigskin, satisfies many people's bloodlust, just as lots of guys—and quite a few girls—enjoy sitting in an arena as a couple of pugilists pound the bejesus out of each other.

There is little or no violence in Major League Baseball, so why do many people love it so much?

They love it because it's such a *skilled* game, and because so many of the men who buy tickets and sit in the stands, or watch the games on TV, have played often enough, at least as boys, to respect how difficult hitting is. I've tried to imagine staying in the batter's box as Dwight Gooden, Roger Clemens or Randy Johnson fired a blazing fastball at a target inches from me, and I'm wearing only a helmet to protect me should the ball hit me. What's more, I'm supposed to hit that ball at just the right moment so that it sails over the wall for a home run.

Imagine doing that over 800 times, the way Barry Bonds did.

But getting back to golf: If the sponsors suddenly

departed, the PGA would end, too. But that won't happen anytime soon. Why not? Because golf, like baseball, requires skill that most people lack, and those who do it often as amateurs, like the armchair baseball players, envy those of us who do it well enough to be professionals.

Look at it this way: that dimpled ball is tiny, that green is sure vast, and that cup way down there is so small that they had to put a flag in it so the golfer can see it. So, here's a club; the golfer must put his little dimpled ball on this thing that's not much bigger than a toothpick, then hit it the ball with one of his skinny clubs until it ends up in that little cup. How many shots do you think he'll need? Four, five?

As screwy as it all is or sounds, I am delighted to be a PGA member. I discovered golf while still a child. I saw the pro golfers on TV and in magazines; they all wore natty shirts, pleated slacks and spiked shoes; none of them ever had cruddy hands or a sore back like workingmen did.

I thought, 'Wow! Sign me up for that!'

I also thought that if I were a golf pro, it really didn't matter if I wasn't an Arnold Palmer or Jack

Nicklaus. If I made enough money just by playing golf, I would probably never have a truly shitty day, unlike most people, whose truly shitty workdays were many and close together.

So, throughout my childhood and years of school, even in high school, when we really had to think seriously about careers and other big stuff, I took maybe two minutes to decide I wanted to play golf.

Of course, I know all about the economy and the rest of the real world: Doctors, lawyers, engineers, realtors. Shit is made, bought and sold; people earn money and spend it; some people work very rarely or not at all, while others work 60 to 100 hours per week, and sometimes those people who work 100 hours per week make less money and get less satisfaction than those working 40 hours per week.

Considering all that, I thought that playing golf for a living, as I've said, meant I didn't have to work for a living.

When a pro golfer plays well, the reporters invite him into the press tent to talk about his performance. The reporters want the golfer to say something quotable. Tiger Woods provides them with plenty for their TV and Internet reports.

I did my best during my visit to the press tent at Placid Oaks, my first visit there as a competitor at the Canadian Open. I had played at the Open a number of times, just as I had played in most of the other major tournaments. But during past Canadian Opens, mostly what they said about me was this:

"Also here, although struggling, is Bayporte native Teddy Crossley…"

I knew some of the reporters, and they knew me, because I had been a tournament player for close to a decade, and some of those sports reporters were astute enough to work in a big market like Bayporte. But to most of those media guys, I was just Also Ran Crossley, another plodding pro who showed up, played his ass off and occasionally won a minor tournament.

Most of the time. to mention Teddy Crossley in the same sentence as Tiger Woods, Rory McIlroy or Phil Mickelson would be an insult to those guys. Even to compare me to Troy Frisby, one of my best friends and always a genuine contender at the Canadian

Open, would be unfair to Troy.

After I told the reporters about how exhilarated I'd felt watching my ball go into the hole instead of the water, especially as I played in front of my countrymen, the media people wanted some personal information about me, mainly because, due to my mediocre career, nobody covering the sport had ever troubled himself to find out who the hell I was. So the reporters asked me to tell them about myself as I sat there on the platform and could hear my voice boom out through the microphone. I took a sip of beer as I looked out at a few dozen guys staring at me as they rested their hands on MacBook Pro laptops.

"Woods, Mickelson and McIlroy like me," I said, startled by my amplified voice and the reporters' bemused typing of my flippant words. "Because I make them look so good."

They didn't laugh, so I threw them a few more goodies. "As for my career highlights, I won the Halitosis Invitational and the Nocturnal Enuresis Classic a few years back."

They asked me to spell enuresis, so I did, and after looking it up online, they exploded in embarrassed laughter.

I told them, as they probably already knew, that I had been born in Bayporte General Hospital, not ten miles away.

"The All-Canadian City," I boasted, "home of the mighty Tyson River, the toque and torrential rain."

I said there were many distinguished native Bayporters in the world, though I couldn't think of any, and that my city felt proud of how few Bayporters had tried to drown themselves in the Tyson River lately.

I explained that I had taught myself golf on one of my city's oldest public courses, Beaver Hills. There I had learned about bad weather, mean dogs, loose women and hustling money from clumsy golfers.

"I guess I feel honored to be competing against Tiger Woods and Phil Mickelson," I said, shrugging.

For whatever reason, I added that I was on my third marriage. Like that was any of their business.

One of the reporters asked me how I felt about competing against my pal Troy Frisby, who had also shot well that day.

The other reporters nodded. They had a potential

story: two good friends, Crossley and Frisby, both leaders in the Canadian Open.

"Yes," I said, "we're good friends, but this tournament is still undecided. If Troy and I start playing badly and slip down, you guys are going to forget us right away and concentrate on the new leaders. That's sort of your job, right?

"Troy was one of the first guys I met when I started touring. We each saw some ability in the other, and we got to hustling the other players for a few bucks."

Yes, we golfers place bets, especially on practice rounds.

"Troy and I have traveled together. Sometimes our wives come with us. But he's a different kind of golfer. He's been here and won this Open and a few other majors. He's more like Tiger, Rory and Phil, an elite golfer. Shit, man, Troy is almost at the point where he needs an entourage to travel with him and take care of the small details. I'm surprised Oprah didn't invite him on her show."

Seriously, what could I tell them about my friendship with Troy? We got along fine, sure, but we started to chill towards each other when we were hanging out in a bar or someplace and one of the big guns like Tiger or Phil recognized him, but not me, and invited him, but not me, over for a drink or a meal.

Troy and I first met in Los Angeles, where we were competing in the Southern California Open. I had just turned pro. I stood there at the practice tee, whacking the hell out of balls, and he clearly saw some potential in me because he actually came up and spoke to me.

"Got a hustle?" he asked. He didn't introduce himself or ask for my name. He obviously assumed I recognized him.

"Nope," I replied.

"I've got one this afternoon. Thomas and Bernard. You want to fleece them with me?"

I knew of them. Don Thomas and Tom Bernard were middling players who had been around for a few years. "What do you have in mind?"

"I'll shake them down," he said. "You just make sure you sink your putts."

"I sank them all yesterday."

"Yesterday means jackshit. You look like you might be able to hit the ball pretty hard. Show me what you can do with that driver."

I smashed a ball out into the distance.

"Not so bad," he said.

I shrugged. "Good enough."

"You're Canadian, eh?" he asked.

I nodded. "I'm from Bayporte."

"I grew up in Toronto," Troy said. "I played in Bayporte last year. Placid Oaks. The Canadian Open."

"I remember. You nearly won."

"Nearly. I'm still pissed off about that," he said. "Next time, I'm going to win the damn thing."

We introduced ourselves and shook hands, then we got into the details of how to hustle Thomas and Bernard. We did them much as planned and pocketed a few thousand dollars of their money.

"What are you doing for dinner?" Troy asked me.

"Make me an offer," I said.

"Want to party with me tonight? We can pick up some lonely flight attendants."

"Let's do it," I said.

He smiled. "I might have fun hanging out with you, especially when our old ladies are away."

We went to a huge bar in Hermosa Beach. It had a spacious dance floor, a dreadful band and beautiful women of all colors.

I sat and drank Canadian Comfort over ice and listened as Troy told sob stories to many women who said they were named Lisa or Jennifer. Troy told them his wife "Laurie" had died of cancer or diabetes or something, or that she'd been crippled up by Lou Gehrig's disease. (They said, "Who's Lou Gehrig?")

Our night climaxed, so to speak, at some girl's beachfront studio apartment as she rode Troy on her sofa. I fixed breakfast for us the next morning.

"I'm in love with her," Troy muttered to me. "Is she Lisa or Jennifer? Damned if I can remember."

"The only name that matters is Laurie. She's your wife." I winked at him.

"Laurie's a damned good woman, too," he said.

From then on, if Troy and I were at the same golf tournament, we spent most of our time together. We got along just fine despite the fact that Troy had only two interests in life, golf and sex. Compared to him, I felt like some sort of Renaissance Man.

In the press tent at Placid Oaks, the reporters asked me about my home life. I told them that Nancy and I had been married a couple of years. I added that she had been in my gallery, the blonde in the halter that couldn't have blocked a sneeze. In her flimsy halter, too-short denim shorts and oversized sunglasses (especially in the overcast Bayporte sky) she could have passed for a porn queen going incognito.

When Nancy and I were first married, Troy told me, "You'll have to play golf in Canada or leave her at home when you travel abroad, because Nancy will have to declare duty on those collector's items or they'll be confiscated at the border."

My first wife, Helga Wark, I told the reporters at Placid Oaks, had been a souvenir from high school. I had married my second wife, Bronwen Morgan, out of simple boredom.

"Bronwen was rich, smart and interested in me, so I said, 'OK. I do,'" I confided to the world. "After my divorce from her, I came away with the impression that the only kind of man who could stay married to her was a poet and philosopher who spent his weekends as a carpenter and handyman.

"Nancy has helped my golf game a great deal. She travels with me, even to places like Thunder Bay and Toledo. She has learned as much about golf as she can.

"I said to Troy and some other guys one day, 'There is no substitute for having a good woman in your life. The better your wife, the better your golf game.'"

We all agreed that the top golfers had good women in their lives. Tiger Woods, too, though we didn't talk about him and his divorce.

I didn't tell the reporters that a bad wife was worse than an uneven golf swing. Helga, my first wife, had very little interest in my golf game aside from how much money I could win that she could spend, but during our marriage, of course, I was just a golf hustler in Bayporte.

Helga, a pretty young thing from Oliver Johnson Secondary School, was ebullient and sweet-natured but terminally horny.

I'd split up with Helga before turning pro.

Well, the woman who, throughout our marriage, made me question my value as a human being, was Bronwen Morgan. A man should not marry a woman who believes she is inherently superior to her husband.

Whenever Bronwen went on tour with me, she criticized everything about me, from my style of dress to my choice of friends. During those times, I probably went on more long, solitary walks than the mailman.

Not to brag, but I've always played golf moderately well, even as a kid teeing off in Beaver Hills. I'd played it with enough success in minor places across Canada to get enough money together so I wouldn't have to go beating the millionaire bushes for sponsor money.

I have survived, too, without having to pimp myself out as a golf instructor. I've always pitied people who were in the unfortunate position of having to try to learn something from me.

Fortunately, I even made friends with superior golfers like Troy Frisby.

After hustling others players for thousands of dollars, I thought that, even if I failed to turn pro, I could play golf for the rest of my life. I would need to live frugally and eat only once or twice per day.

When I did turn pro, I won some minor money right away. I did so without anyone's help, and felt gratified that, for the time being, I didn't have to go back to Bayporte to kiss the rich guys' butts so they would sponsor me and take half—or more—of my winnings.

Sponsorship often is the only option for a young, indigent player. The sponsor will give the youngster a credit card and enough cash to live comfortably, and at the end of the year, they will do the accounting: how much the youngster spent, how much he won, etc. Ideally, the sponsor will withdraw his assistance once the golfer has become financially self-reliant.

The youngster will show a profit, loss or he will break even; regardless, the sponsor gains something, even if only a tax deduction. Plus, the youngster gets some visibility from being on the tour.

When I told people that I wanted to start touring, they told other people and soon I met Aldo Chies, a

Bayporte mining tycoon, who invited me to lunch at Placid Oaks. We had a few cocktails and he told me he considered himself a decent golf player but a far better mining tycoon. He laughed, and so did I.

"Teddy," he said, "you're a good golfer, but there are plenty of good golfers around. Know what I mean?"

"I hear ya."

"You're probably the best I've seen around here, but that doesn't mean much. Have you played outside of western Canada at all?"

I shrugged. "Ontario and Alberta, but that's all."

"Those golf tours go everywhere," he said.

"Absolutely."

"Let me talk straight to you. Teddy, you can hit the ball as hard as Tiger and a lot of those other guys, and that's a good thing, especially since you're only of moderate physical size. But you can hit the ball a mile. I've heard you can beat the shit out of everybody at Beaver Hills. Is that so?"

"Beaver Hills doesn't attract many quality golfers."

He laughed. "I guess not." Then, "Teddy, I have faith in you. I believe you are a golfer who can do big things, and I want to help you out."

"Tell me more."

"I want to give you my American Express card so that when you go to a major tournament, you have no financial worries. You just eat prime rib, drink Canadian Comfort over ice and play good golf."

"Nice work if you can get it," I said. "But I'd want to do something for you in return."

"Oh!" He laughed. "I'm in it for the thrill of seeing a fellow Canuck dazzle the world. But if you started winning some serious cash, I'd just take the usual sixty-forty split."

I swallowed. "Sixty to you?"

He nodded. "But don't worry about *that*. Just eat well, get plenty of rest and play good golf."

I stood up. "Well, Aldo, I certainly appreciate your desire to help me, but I think I manage things on my own."

"Listen, Teddy, if you change your mind about this, just remember you can always find me here."

I told him that I wouldn't change my mind.

Aldo had already forgotten me and was shouting to someone at another table about some mining operations in the Northwest Territories.

The closest I have ever come to requiring sponsorship or any other kind of practical help came during my marriage to Brownen Morgan. Bronwen, a fine woman, should have known better than to marry a professional golfer.

She wanted to broaden my horizons; I wanted to keep them narrow. She said I had fallen far short of my potential; I agreed with her—I wanted to be the finest golfer around. She said that my potential had nothing to do with golf. In our three years of marriage, I kept wondering what, and who, she wanted me to become, and why she didn't just let up and back off when her efforts to change me just made us both miserable.

After a time, I knew that golf hadn't broken us up. We'd done it to ourselves. I grew sick of traveling, practicing, competing and listening to Bronwen as she quizzed me on the day's events and sneered at my ignorant responses.

We shared an apartment in Bayporte, our native city. Several Canadian pro golfers reside there, mainly because its airport never gets snowed in and the city, expensive as it is, is a slightly cheaper alternative to Toronto.

On the day I moved out of our apartment, Bronwen had been trying to goad me into sticking up for our hometown.

"You're always such a Bayporte-basher," she complained as I loaded my possessions into the trunk of my car.

"It's a snobbish, snooty city with sports teams that never win anything," I retorted. "And the last time I went to the zoo, it reeked of feces."

She changed the subject. "Why are you giving up on *us* so quickly?"

"Because," I replied, "we shouldn't have gotten married to begin with."

I suppose I felt distracted during the Canadian Open because Bronwen got sick. Just as I start getting my shit together for a major tournament, my ex, whom I do not hate, and in many ways really quite like, tells me that she is having a huge problem with her lungs.

Bronwen and I got along much better after our

divorce, and she became a true friend following my marriage to Nancy. I suppose that was the key to my relationship with Bronwen: no longer burdened by being husband and wife, we lightened up and became close friends.

On the road somewhere, immersed in my sport, I had received a call from her about how she had started getting severe medical problems. So she had gone to the doctor, and he'd ordered tests and given her some bad news.

I had no idea what to say. Bronwen had just turned 30.

"Let's not freak out or anything," I'd told her. "They have treatments for everything these days…"

"Maybe I should give up heroin and cocaine," she said, cackling.

Nancy cared little about Bronwen's medical crisis. I think I understood why: Nancy's family, overworked, underpaid service providers, resented the privileges of moneyed people like Bronwen.

"Let her spend some of that bread on getting the best doctors and hospitals," Nancy said. "If they can't save her, too fuckin' bad."

HOLE IN ONE

2

Bayporte, my home and native land, is where I met all three of my wives. I'd leave town so often to go on tour to so many distant locations—all over North America and beyond—and, while living in hotels and meeting people on and off the golf course, I'd try to seduce many women and succeed sometimes. So I felt surprised that, after divorcing Number Two and getting laid in diverse places, I met Number Three half an hour from my condo.

Troy, a few other guys and I decided to drive out east to Carol's Place, a funky hangout by the Tyson River. Carol's Place used to be a shady, forbidding bar called the Lookout, where bikers sold cocaine and crystal meth, killed debtors and snitches and dumped their bodies into the river.

Over time, the Canadian National Police raided the Lookout too often, so the bikers did their deals elsewhere. The bar closed and reopened. Now, as Carol's Place, it had been reborn as an R&B joint with nightly live music.

"I want to go there," Troy said, "because it used to be the Lookout. Even in Toronto we knew about its raids and arrests. I just want to be able to say I was there."

So we followed the river all the way out to the suburb of Cornwall, where it smelled swampy, and sat down to hear some live music.

Carol's Place still seemed rugged to me, hulking under a bridge, its neon sign blazing in the darkness. Only a rusted-out chain-link fence separated the nightclub from the shore of the river.

At Carol's Place, as at the Lookout, a man wouldn't go inside wearing pretty clothes. The tough guys in there might be offended by a fancy gentleman and give him a hard time.

The featured singer that evening, Nancy Parrish, came on stage, direct from her engagement as a server at the Tally-ho Tavern a dozen blocks away. While she would never make the world forget Barbra Streisand, she kept us all entertained with a number of classics no singer could murder.

I'd drunk enough liquid courage to write Nancy a little note inviting her to our table for a drink. I gave our server five dollars to deliver the message, and Nancy, between sets, bounded over and plopped onto a free seat. She made us howl with the number of naughty words she knew and how many of them she could fit into one sentence. Also, she owned two of the finest of breasts I had ever seen.

Nancy paid most of her attention to Troy. Women usually did. They had seen him on TV and even bothered to remember his name. I just happened to be some guy he was with.

When she went back on stage, Nancy pointed at us and introduced us to the audience, which relieved me because some of the factory workers and stevedores were sneering at Troy's linen jacket and perhaps needed reassurance that he wasn't a fairy.

Before we left, we gave her a tournament badge and parking permit and insisted she come on out and watch us play golf. She asked what she should wear, and we said to wear whatever she found comfy in muggy weather.

So naturally she showed up in a tiny halter-and-shorts outfit that probably scandalized the entire country club. I felt so distracted by her mostly naked presence that I finished over par on every hole and ended up next to last for the tournament.

Nancy yawned a lot out there and smoothed her hair. She looked around and shrugged. Back in the clubhouse, over cocktails she said, "It's so bloody *quiet* out there, like they're doing brain surgery. Why aren't they hooting and hollering?"

She looked around. "There aren't any Bayporte Bullies or Invaders around. Too bad. Have you met those guys? They're lots of fun!"

For several minutes she stared at the old men in blazers and white shirts who pretty much ran things there at Placid Oaks. I couldn't really fault her if she felt that she was sitting in a really fancy geriatric hospital.

Suddenly she yelled, "Hey, everybody, let's have some fun! You have but one shot at life and when you're dead you're done!"

Then she told Troy and me a few old jokes about "Pakis" and "faggots."

At one point, as Nancy sat telling us one of her jokes, an old man approached our table. His name was Larry Rawson, and he had gotten filthy rich by extracting tons of gold, silver and other shit from the Canadian soil. He had also been the golf tournament's chairman for the past decade or so. If you were a celebrity, or a rich guy, or both, you would probably consider Larry Rawson one of your best friends in Bayporte.

"Young lady," he said when he reached our table, "I need to tell you that your behavior is just a tiny bit boisterous."

Nancy, in the middle of one of her jokes, flicked her eyes in his direction for a split second and said, "Eat me. Grandpa." Then she went on with her joke.

At first, Rawson looked befuddled, as if he hadn't heard her, or, if he had, he missed the meaning of her words. But then he sorted it out and smiled, as if appreciating her sassiness. He also saw her breasts, and he walked away, apparently pleased to have someone like her among all those rich old white bastards.

I knew immediately that I wanted Nancy. I accept, even if I don't especially like, how a woman's physical beauty obsesses me. I have always been a fool for the pretty ones.

I invited her to join me on the tour. When she reminded me of her own professional aspirations as a diva, I told her, as diplomatically as possible, that I could show her a much better time than those bubbas at Carol's Place. She agreed that, as a vocalist, she was going nowhere fast. She took no offense at what I'd said and said that she could leave town indefinitely and nobody at Carol's Place, or anywhere else, would notice her absence.

I explained to her that I was between relationships, was interested in nobody but her, I had a big Volvo with satellite radio. Furthermore, I drove or flew to places like Pebble Beach, Augusta and others, that offered plenty of comforts for a young lady like herself.

I added, truthfully, that I was still married to Bronwen but we would soon file for divorce. I did not lie to Nancy; I told her that my marriage had lasted a few years, but ours had been mostly a confusing and frustrating union.

"Bronwen is a fine woman," I explained, "but what did we have in common? She hates golf and thinks it's a colossal waste of time. Of course, she says the same about most other things, too.

"She is a desirable woman if you get turned on by anorexic-looking ladies who always wear black turtlenecks, green corduroy slacks and have this thing for reading highbrow magazines like *The New Yorker* and *Esquire*."

"Quite a mystery why you two got married," Nancy said.

"Tell me about it. I think one of the reasons was simple loneliness. People think of a golf tournament as a party atmosphere, which it often is, but there's also a great deal of loneliness when you don't have that special someone to share it all with. Also, with Bronwen, I got as much nooky as I wanted. But with her, it was like banging my teacher. She never shut up, even in bed.

"Of course, in her mind, I had have a few redeeming qualities. I didn't have any use for Bayporte, which made two of us, and I didn't have much use for people with wealth and power, and she liked that, too.

"Really, when you think about it, the only reason she married me was to have someone she could make fun of. Bronwen really thought I was some kind of retard, and whenever she found one of my golf magazines or videos lying around, well, she just couldn't resist mocking me."

Being in a talkative mood, I then told Nancy about Helga Wark, my first wife. Like Brownen, Helga had remained in Bayporte, and we were the best of friends.

"But Helga and me? Shit, that was so long ago, and we were such kids, that it's hard for me to remember what went through our minds when we were together." I chuckled. "I must be a decent-enough bastard because my ex-wives still like me."

Nancy smiled. "Well, if I'm going to be Number Three, I just hope there won't be a Number Four."

So she went with me, on the road, to amuse herself while I played golf.

"I'm grateful for anything that will get me out of fuckin' Bayporte for a while," she said.

I went everywhere with Nancy and enjoyed looking at people's faces as they checked us out.

'Hi,' I'd say to the golfers' wives, 'how are you, I'd like you to meet Nancy from Bayporte. Bronwen? Oh, we're still married, but she's got a lung tumor or something so we're getting a divorce. Nancy is my main squeeze now. Doesn't she have the greatest pair of zoomers you've ever seen?'

One of our first adventures together was a trip to Europe. I think that's what you're supposed to do after you've split up with your wife and are starting all over again with someone new; you go to fun places together, have long talks and memorable experiences. Plus, I really wanted to walk around with Nancy on my arm and watch the world ogle her zoomers.

I chose Europe, and Britain in particular, because of the British Open. Every golfer wants to compete in that event, and that year they were having it at St. Edwards, which must be one of the world's most challenging courses. I doubted I could come close to winning there but felt eager to get a look at that big green bastard anyway.

We landed at Heathrow and stayed in a fine old hotel. I made the smart decision to bring along three good friends: MasterCard, VISA and American Express.

I also got us a car and driver, rather than rent a car and try to enjoy the sights with Nancy while I drove on the wrong side of the road.

London, as Nancy most astutely noted, certainly was different from Canada and the States.

She fell in love with London's shops and bought enough shit to open her own store back home.

Nancy loved listening to the people's authentic British accents.

"Hip-hip, cheerio, hullo love." She threw back her head and laughed. "Those fuckers don't know how funny they sound."

I discovered bangers, mash and ale, so my stomach stayed full. I got in a few days of practice at St. Eddie's, which, alas, had heather growing in some areas, and a hotel on the course, so if my shot went really wild it might hit one of the golfers' wives as she watched the action from her balcony.

On the evening before the tournament, I wanted to take it nice and easy, maybe make a few alterations to my clubs or just watch British sitcoms on TV with Nancy. But then I checked my emails and found a message from Helga, my first wife. My girlfriend at Sir Oliver Johnson Secondary, she was now a moderately classy prostitute and the only person I had ever encountered who drank Canadian Comfort with Mountain Dew.

Helga had hovered out there in my world, occasionally sending me emails for money she wanted to use to get out of "the life" and get into something "legal and productive."

Helga Wark, someone I knew very well when she and I were very young, remains someone close to my heart and prominent in my mind, even if I wished otherwise.

We were a high school couple who got married because she said she was pregnant, and although no child was ever actually born (perhaps because none had ever been conceived), we stayed married for a while and enjoyed ourselves and each other as often as not. To complicate things, she had four brothers who would have made fine Al Qaeda terrorists.

I had deep feelings for Helga, even though she was immoral, outrageous, profane and entirely too generous with her pussy. But she was also pretty, exuberant, vivacious, wonderfully spontaneous and eager to be loved, or at least liked. In retrospect, I'd have to say she wasn't the object of my adoration; I was young and naive and innocent, and she turned me on with her "Fuck tomorrow, let's live for today" free-spiritedness.

I also would have a very difficult time forgetting her brothers, as much as I would like to do so.

Willy, the oldest, was certainly the meanest. The others were Robby, Joel, Dave and Kelly.

Helga and Rob were twins, as were Joel and Dave. Kelly was the youngest, and all those Wark boys were as ornery, territorial and unforgiving as any bunch of suburban bullies and sadists you'd ever avoided on a dark street.

The Wark brothers all lifted weights; they had

Arnold Schwarzenegger necks and wrists. They wore crew cuts and sleeveless T-shirts. Pallid and freckled, they avoided sunlight and seldom smiled. If anyone ever wondered about just how tough the Warks really were, he just had to watch the brothers compete in the Bayporte Golden Gloves. Each of the Wark brothers, stepping into the ring, was so buffed out, pale and, well, crazy-looking, like an idiot country boy from a Hollywood movie, that his opponent would frown, as if wanting to ask, *Do I really have to fight this cracker?*

The Wark in the ring would fight like Mike Tyson, scarcely looking at the other pugilist but burrowing in and throwing pulverizing punches that ended bouts quickly.

Throughout our childhoods, I was the Warks' friend, to the extent that they had any; and as their teammate, I had little concern that they would start in on me once they felt the urge to terrorize our community. Of course, if their usual targets—Jews, Pakis, sissies, fat kids—were unavailable, they weren't above hassling a friend.

The Warks had fun humiliating local guys who

were sitting with their dates in cars parked outside fast food joints. You might find a Wark tapping on your window; you would wind it down because keeping it up would be suicidal.

When he ordered you to step out of your car, you would comply, and shake with terror when he told you to get naked; your date would probably freak out that this Neanderthal was going to rape her after he got done with you.

Once you were in your birthday suit, Wark would press a ten-dollar bill into your hand and say, "Go have some supper." He meant, of course, that he wanted you to walk, stark naked, into the McDonald's or Burger King twenty feet away and order a meal.

You knew you didn't really have the option of saying no, so you would do this. Your head would spin and your body perspire profusely as you half-ran into the lobby, and then you might faint or have a panic attack as the counter workers looked away, their faces nearly as red as yours.

Or maybe Wark wanted only to fight, and he would pound on your window until you and your date started shrieking at each other. When a Wark pounded on my window, I got out immediately, gave him the fight he wanted—I mostly just covered up and let him pound away at me—then shook his hand and smiled.

"Good fight, Robby," I said, "and nice to see you again."

One time, Willy and Joel actually took over our entire high school.

They liked to get drunk at Paul's Submarine Stop, where Paul reluctantly served them beer with their sandwiches because they threatened to firebomb his business if he refused to let them drink. I loved to eat at Paul's because he would grill the bread, cheese and the result was a uniquely tasty sandwich. In all my travels, even in the most celebrated eateries, I have yet to find anything nearly as good.

Anyway, Willy and Joel, pissed on lunchtime beer, staggered from Paul's to school and headed directly for the principal's office. The office staff, as terrified of the Warks as anyone could be, stepped aside as Joel held a knife to the throat of Mr. Barnes, the principal, and gave him a choice: sit still or die.

Willy went into the booth next to Barnes' office

where the school kept its public address system. He turned on the microphone and spoke to everyone on all three floors of Canada's largest high school.

Helga and I were in the library. I had my arm around her waist and my mind not at all on my studies. People knew that my girlfriend was the only sister of the most insufferable bullies in the entire school. They thought I was completely brave, or totally stupid, to be dating her.

We suddenly stopped groping each other as we heard the P.A. system crackle a bit and then heard the unmistakable voice of Willy.

"Attention, everyone at Oliver Johnson Secondary School…"

Helga and I looked at each other, like, *Uh-oh, what's he up to now?*

"I'm broadcasting this message to tell you that there's been a change of management at this school. I'm the boss now, and I want the following people to meet me downstairs in the boiler room in fifteen minutes…" He said the names of several students and teachers, all of them pretty young women. Nobody needed to guess why he wanted to be alone with them downstairs.

Throughout his broadcast, he giggled and guffawed.

"Oh, yeah," Willy added, "from now on, there's no more science, English or social studies. It will be all sex education and sports, and the girls will have to show up at the gym with no panties on."

Willy laughed so hard he could barely speak. With nothing more to say, he turned off the microphone and went to class.

Were he and Joel arrested, or at least expelled, over these antics? Certainly not. Barnes, like everyone else, feared the entire Wark family far too much ever to come down hard on any of them; besides, they were remarkable athletes. Willy, easily the best running back the school had had in years, was nearly as good as my cousin, Red Crossley, who became a football stud at Northup University and then went pro. But of course nobody would tell Willy that anyone was better at anything than he was. I certainly wouldn't.

Ultimately, all Barnes could do to them was make them apologize to the entire school during an assembly. Willy and Joel stood onstage at the microphone, their hands on their hips in defiant postures, and Willy said, "Mr. Barnes said we did a bad thing and we need to say we're sorry. We were just goofing around and didn't mean to offend anyone. So me and Joel are gonna try and not drink so much bloody beer and we'll try to start mindin our manners. That's all I got to say."

Then the two boys scratched their temples with their middle fingers, a gesture their audience greeted with laughter and cheers.

Soon after high school. Willy lost half his right leg by being stupid. He and his brothers, after procuring mace cans somehow, drove around squirting passersby. This wasn't the ordinary "pepper spray" that cops use now; no, this was *real* mace, the nerve gas/tear gas compound that the cops probably aren't allowed to use any longer. I am ashamed to report that I sat in their car and cheered them on as they had their retarded fun.

Willy, although he had no way of knowing it, would endure hospitalization and amputation that evening, and the reason was that his brother Kelly made the dreadful mistake of leaning out of the car and spraying mace on the wrong guy standing on the sidewalk outside the Nite Cap bar. The guy he sprayed was Ahab the Arab.

Ahab the Arab, a few years our senior, had become a legend in our Bayporte neighborhood. Ahab was the type who, when he went into a bar, pool hall or other tough-guy hangout, would find everyone, even career criminals wanted on Canada-wide warrants, smiling and getting out if his way.

Everyone tacitly acknowledged Ahab the Arab as the meanest of the Bayporte badasses. The only things people actually knew about him were that he was tall and muscular, had a shiny moustache, had a mean-looking smile that he used when he got mad, and that he had gotten into trouble in Montreal or somewhere else back east, which was probably why he had come to Bayporte. His real name was Ayub Khan. He was a Pakistani, not an Arab.

Willy, of course, knew about Ahab, and vice versa, but the two hadn't fought because one of them would have to lose.

When Joel pulled up to the sidewalk in front of the Nite Cap and Kelly sprayed a long, thick stream of mace on the back and shoulders of some black-haired man wearing a plaid work shirt, none of us saw his victim and were too busy pointing and chuckling to care much about the sorry goof and his ruined work shirt.

But then we heard a deep voice yell, "What the fuck—!" and realized, at the same moment, that we'd just gotten into some big trouble.

We were in a car; Ahab the Arab was on foot. We should have driven off into the night, but Willy muttered, "Let me out. I can take him. I can do it."

"It's Ahab the Arab!" I whispered, horrified. "You sprayed Ahab! Now he's gonna kill us!"

"Let's fuck him up," said Joel. "Let's kick his ass."

"No," said Willy. "Just me and him. Two hits: me hitting him and him hitting the ground."

"How about Joel hitting the gas pedal," I said, "and us getting the fuck out of here?"

Ahab the Arab started yelling at us.

"Willy Wark! You're in that car with all your bum

buddies to protect you, eh? Get *out* here, you fuckin goof—"

Willy sprang out of the car and slammed into Ahab the Arab. The two toughest guys in town went at it in what I had considered the unthinkable yet inevitable Bayporte brawl. They mixed it up for close to half an hour. Both guys scored knockdowns and got puffy faces. They kicked and scratched; they tried to knee each other's scrotum but missed. They wrestled on the pavement but got nowhere.

The fight ended when Willy, enraged at being unable to incapacitate his opponent, threw a roundhouse punch that ended up putting a dent in a streetlamp. Willy bent over, howling in agony, shaking his injured hand. Ahab stepped up, punched him in the face twice as Willy tried to defend himself, feebly, with his one good hand. Then Ahab picked him up, Hulk Hogan-style, and threw him through the plate-glass window of Gook's Cambodian Café. Willy, a shard of glass sticking out of his right leg, lay motionless as the ambulance arrived. Willy healed up fast, but lost his right leg from the knee down.

Around town, they said that Ahab the Arab won

the "ultimate fight." But had he really? By fighting Willy, Ahab had declared war on the whole Wark family. They would come looking for him.

Joel Wark soon found Ahab the Arab in a downtown video arcade, sneaked up on him as Ahab the Arab played Pac-Man, shot him the back of the head with a .45 automatic and sauntered off.

The Bayporte police, relieved to be ridden of Ahab the Arab and his macho bullshit, called the murder a "gang-related shooting" and said nothing more. Also, Joel had a great chance of winning the Provincial high-jump competition, so why arrest him over the murder of a notorious troublemaker like Ahab the Arab?

Soon after having his leg partly amputated, Willy got a prosthesis and taught himself to walk on it so naturally that everyone could scarcely believe his right leg was half fake. He even won a scholarship to Northup as a shot-putter and discus-thrower. If he hadn't lost half that leg in that fight, he'd have gone to the U. as a football player.

As Willy learned to live with his prosthesis, he worked part-time at his father's all-night takeout joint,

Freddy's Pizza 2 Go. He stood at the counter at four in the morning when a couple of Chinese gangsters emerged from a black BMW. One of them waved a .38 revolver in Willy's indignant face while another demanded the contents of his cash register.

Willy responded by telling them how he felt about the way "Chinks" had taken over his city, and said that if they didn't get the fuck out of his restaurant immediately, he would kick their yellow asses all the way back to Hong Kong.

The guy with the .38 shot Willy once in the chest, but that just made the Wark boy angrier. He snatched the gun away from the gangster, unfastened his prosthesis and whacked them both in the face until they lay bloodied and unconscious on the tile floor.

Willy called the police. "This is the manager of Freddy's on West Broadway. I've been shot a couple of times, so you better send an ambulance." He looked down at the injured gangsters and added, "I also got two dickless pieces of shit layin on my floor, so you also better send a hearse or something because I don't think they're gonna make it."

Whenever I get to thinking about the Wark family,

I start wishing I had never dated Helga nor hung out with her crazy-mean brothers. During my marriage to Bronwen, I amused her for endless hours with my stories about life around the Warks, and she asked myriad questions about my feelings towards them, as if I'd married into a Colombian crime family. She wondered why she had never heard of them on the TV news. Ahab the Arab? He sounded like some sort of mythical character out of our most colorful folklore. Had he *really* thrown Willy through the glass of that restaurant at the conclusion of their fight? And Joel! Walking into that arcade and shooting Ahab? Or Willy beating the shit out of those Chinese gangsters during the botched robbery? Why hadn't she heard about any of that in the news?

Nancy seemed much less interested in the Warks and their exploits. She asked no questions and rolled her eyes. "Why don't you *not* tell me about them? I didn't go to Oliver Johnson High, but I still had to put up with my share of punks, bullies and sadists. I've tried to forget about those lowlifes ever since."

I thought about Helga, Bronwen and Nancy for a few minutes as I sat in our London hotel room and went through my emails. I read Helga's to Nancy:

Teddy Boy,

Didn't expect to hear from your first love while you're out there with your latest flame in jolly old England, eh? I would love to get on a plane and just zoom off to someplace distant and exciting but I've been stuck here in rainy old Bayporte and it really just kind of sucks all the time.

Teddy, I guess you know that I've done OK in general with "the world's oldest profession" since our divorce, but lately things haven't been so good. I don't know if it's the economy or what, but my clients just haven't been requiring my services often enough for me to maintain an adequate standard of living. I'm wondering if you could spare $10,000 so that I can get into another business. With high technology, I could set up an Internet sex service. This kind of thing has been done with much success in cities all over the world and I have a few ideas about how mine could be better than everyone else's. in fact. If you could spare $15,000 that would be even better because I have some expenses here and there that I need to take care of.

I suppose you are disappointed in my way of earning a living since our divorce, but I see it as a public service I provide, and everyone needs to get his rocks off now and again.

If you decide you don't want to help me financially, just remember that I know so much about you and the things you would rather forget about, like how you cheated people at Beaver Hills and the illegal activities you and my brothers did way back when. If the public knew about all that, it would do very bad things to your image.

I look forward to hearing from you and that you will do your best for me. Say hi to that big-titted bimbo you've been running around with.

Helga

Nancy didn't like Helga's email. "She's turning tricks in Bayporte and she's calling *me* a 'big-titted bimbo'?"

Then, unbelievably, my iPhone rang and Bronwen was on the line from Bayporte. I said to myself, 'What the fuck? I have an ex's email in front of me, an ex on the phone, and my current woman just ten feet away. How would the other tournament pros handle such a situation?'

"I've been sitting here bored," Bronwen was

saying, "having a couple of drinks, and I started thinking of you. I want to know why you were so rude to me earlier this year in Los Angeles."

"Don't remember seeing you down there," I said.

"Don't you? You were sitting in the bar at the L.A. Grand Sunset Marquis or whatever the fuck it's called. You were with some drunken pros and network honchos when I walked in with some friends and smiled at you, but you just looked away."

"Oh, that was a while ago, Bronnie. Get over it and get remarried. Start life all over again. And find yourself some better friends. Those people at the bar seemed like a motley bunch."

"They were artists."

"Artists are a motley bunch."

"One of them is a world-renowned painter and sculptor of hippopotamuses."

"That right, eh?"

"Don't be a smartass, Ted. It's great that artists are appreciating the beauty of such a misunderstood creature. Hippos are one of the most hated and feared mammals on the planet."

"Hippos are huge, filthy, vicious beasts. They

deserved to be hated," I told her. "Also, this call is expensive as hell. Did you phone me just to argue about hippos?"

"Well, no. It's just that I was having a drink, and I decided to call you and tell you that I never looked down on you because you were a golfer."

"Thank you so much, " I said.

"I just felt it was a shame to see someone devote his entire existence to sticks and balls."

"Well, Bronnie, when we first hooked up and got married, you knew that golf was my livelihood. Anyway, it's all in the past. We need to live in the here and now."

"Yes," she said. "I can recall looking at you and picturing you coming out with your own line of high-end golf apparel. I imagined you modeling slacks and shirts in a *Playboy* ad."

I chuckled.

"People ask me why you and I ever got married, and I tell them the truth: Because you were a fun guy who made me laugh. You didn't wear a suit every day and kiss ass for a living. Say, how's London? On my last trip there, I saw three dozen places where the

Beatles played their first gig."

"London? It is what it is."

Bronwen said, "I was difficult, Ted. I want to apologize. Please forgive me. I should have been more supportive of you. Still, you couldn't blame me for having a hard time getting used to your lifestyle. You know it was pretty unconventional."

"I showed you a good time."

"You took me to lots of places," she said. "But I felt we were culturally deprived."

"Well, we didn't take in much Broadway or Shakespeare. If that's what you wanted, you should have spoken up."

"Ted, you know I've always had a high opinion of you. I admire people who are good at what they do, and you've always been able to make a good living at a highly competitive sport. I felt I could remake you into a larger, freer and more loving person."

"You can't remake a person, Bronnie. Don't you ever listen to the radio shrinks?"

Nancy said, "Tell that crazy bitch to hang up and quit bugging you or I'll throw all your golf clubs into the Thames."

"I heard that," Bronwen said.

"Bronnie," I said, "I'm sure you know about Nancy and me by now. We're in love and I'm going to marry her."

After a few moments of silence, Bronwen said, "Just wondering, Ted: Is Nancy pretty? Does she have a V-8 pussy and a Cadillac ass?"

"Yes, ma'am."

"Ted," she said after a long swallow, "breaking up is a difficult thing for both parties. I have to be single again, and it's doubly hard when everyone knows that my ex is cavorting about with some sexpot like Nancy. Have you stopped to think about how she and you look together? It's just not very respectable. Have you considered your public image?"

"There's only one thing I've been considering lately," I told her, "and that's how to improve my golf swing. I don't care too much if people gawk at Nancy's big boobies or think I'm a dirty old man for screwing her. Once I find my golf swing, I'll get busy with that other existential stuff." Then, "Have you heard anything from the lawyers about finalizing our divorce?"

"Oh, yeah, it's official. I knew I had an adequate reason for calling you. It's a done deal. *We're* a done bloody deal. Does that brighten your day?"

"Thanks for telling me," I said.

"The fine mayor of Bayporte proclaimed this Fuck You Day, so I went and pigged out on fast food and had several Canadian Comforts over ice."

"So now you're fat, drunk and divorced," I said.

Bronwen snorted. "And proud of it." She added, "Ted, seriously, I want to see you when you get back from London. You have some stuff at my place and I'd like to have you as a friend I can talk to. Do you think your fiancée would break your clubs if you had lunch with me?"

"Could be, but I'll call you when I get back." I told her about Helga's email. "I was reading it when you called. Women and girls rule my world."

"You need us." Then, "Did Helga really threaten to go to the sports media about your hustling days if you refused to pay her off? Sounds like a good deal for you. Tiger Woods and John Daly have had their scandals, so maybe you need yours. If the public knew some naughty stuff about you, it might perceive you as a more colorful character."

"I think I'd rather stay boring."

"Hey, you know what, Teddy? Not to brag, but I really look pretty hot these days," she said.

"You weren't so ugly the last time I saw you."

"Hey! You know what might be fun? You go ahead and marry Nancy and I'll be your girlfriend. Check that out with her."

"Maybe," I said.

"I *do* regret that our marriage ended. You know that, right?"

"Yes, Bronnie. But it's better now. We're both going to live much longer."

"I suppose you're right. This call is getting expensive, so I'm going to hang up. But let me leave you with one thought. Remember it as you travel from golf course to golf course, and remind yourself once in a while that you heard it from me first."

"Spill it."

"Don't wear white on the golf course because it makes you look like an albino. Don't wear red, of course, because it's Tiger's color and people will think you're a copycat. Wear navy blue."

Naturally, I did not spend the rest of the evening thinking about St. Edwards and all the challenges that awaited me on that course. No, I spent that evening passionately reassuring Nancy that I did *not* still have deep feelings for my two ex-wives.

Nancy once told me, "The reason you want me is that you have a pervy breast fixation. Your mum must have weaned you too early."

I suppose I played well in London despite the poor weather and my crazy caddy, a Mr. Bean lookalike with bugging-out eyes and a childlike, guileless fascination with everything. He was such a delightful distraction that I couldn't concentrate on my golf game.

I failed to put up a very low number on the board there, and my caddy blamed it on my inability to play on English grass.

"You see, matey," he explained, "you have to *communicate* with our greens before you can win over here."

"How do I do that?" I asked, thinking: *Communicate* with grass? That sounds like something they would say in California. But in California, "grass" has a much different meaning.

"You have to get used to the grass before you can communicate with it," he said.

"Communicate with the ground? That sounds like something they would say in California."

I got to know how to communicate just fine with plenty of English food, but that didn't make my golf game go any better.

When I had a crucial putt to make, I asked Mr. Bean how and where the putt would break.

"Can't tell you, matey," he said. "I mean, I could, but I might be wrong, and I would feel dreadful about it. A nasty little bugger, that."

I didn't get used to that course, and apparently it didn't like me any more than I liked it, so we didn't communicate well and I finished eighth. I believed that I could have won the tournament if, as Mr. Bean said, I'd made friends with the course.

Mostly, I would say, the trip was good rather than bad. The beer tasted like urine, but I was OK with that. Towards the end of our trip, Nancy summed things up like so: "The States has Disneyland and the Statue of Liberty, and we have Whistler and the CN

Tower, but how can we compete with the royal shit that England has?

...

Next, we went to France so I could play in another tournament. Because North America takes its fun so seriously, it always produces more than its share of good or great golf players, and European tournaments always welcome us. They gave us a fancy room at a great hotel in Paris, which really wasn't all that valuable a bribe.

We walked through Paris so that Nancy, a lifelong Doors fan, could have a little cry at the grave of Jim Morrison. Then I went to play at a tournament that I found less challenging than Beaver Hills back in Bayporte. The prize money was less than what I could hustle years earlier.

The crowds were absent, the European competitors had less talent than American golf instructors, and the course itself, whatever they called it, looked like the movie *Caddyshack* after the gopher and Bill Murray were done with it. I think I finished fourth. I could have done better if I'd tried harder.

Our trip home was fast and efficient: Paris to

Toronto to Bayporte. I slept most of the way because air travel makes me drowsy. At Bayporte International Airport, we had a surprise: Brownen had come to meet us.

So there we were, Nancy and me, with Bronwen, and she confronted more than welcomed us. I am an obscure public figure. I can go wherever I want and few or no people will recognize me. No one will ask me for an autograph or cell-phone picture. I get no media attention in foreign or domestic airports.

But there stood Bronwen.

She had called Andrea Frisby and asked about my arrival date. I had called Andrea, too, and asked if she and Troy would put us up for a few days while we recovered from our trip overseas. Ever since splitting up with Bronwen and becoming homeless, I'd camped out in one of Troy and Andrea's guest rooms. I would get my own apartment, naturally, as soon as things slowed down a bit for me and I didn't have to fly everywhere for tournaments. But for the time being, I had a home at the Frisbys' estate, including my guest.

Andrea said very little. She just smiled and nodded,

and otherwise remained a sunny force in the cosmos. Troy didn't want her saying too much, and she often glanced at him before opening her mouth. Andrea and Bronwen were friends, so Andrea didn't mind telling Bronwen about my flight back to Bayporte.

So there I stood, with Nancy at my side and Bronwen in my face. I tried to be funny: "Hello, my name is Bill Gates. Is your network software working OK?"

Then I grabbed Nancy's arm and said to Brownen, "Bronnie, have you ever eaten at Hooters? I'd like you to meet Nancy, its CEO and poster girl."

I'm not sure why I felt so awkward. Bronwen and I were no longer a couple. But then I thought of what Troy Frisby had said about these moments: "If you get caught with the wrong woman on your arm, deny all wrongdoing. And if your denials don't work, burst into tears and beg forgiveness." As an alternative, Troy said, "If they catch you cheating on your wife and there's nothing else you can say, try this: 'I'm just a media consultant from the Midwest, but I'm really flattered that you think I'm Troy Frisby, the golfer. I don't know him personally, but I understand he is a very handsome and talented man.'"

Anyway, Bronwen just stood there looking at the two of us. Then Nancy had her say: "Bronwen, you can stand there all day and half the night looking like we've betrayed you, but the fact is that you had your time with Teddy and now it's over and it's *our* time together. Teddy and I are in love and we want to spend the rest of our lives together and if you don't like it, well, tough titties. Love is a beautiful and precious thing. If you want to be in love again, maybe you should be out there meeting new men instead of obsessing over the one who got away. Teddy's just a man and I'm just a woman and we happen to be a couple. Don't be mad at him just because he likes cute babes and feelin' good."

Bronwen looked at her, then at me, then at her again, as if Nancy had issued some sort of official statement in a foreign language and Brownen looked to me for an interpretation that didn't happen. Finally, Brownen just put her hands on her hips and said one word:

"Fuck."

"So, Bronnie," I said at last, "do you have some

business here at the airport besides giving Nancy and me a hard time?"

"I wanted to see you, and I had a feeling you wouldn't call me while you were in town—"

"He wasn't going to," Nancy said.

"So I figured it was catch you at the airport or not catch you at all." Then, "Let's meet up for a drink and a talk. You still have some stuff at my place that you need to pick up. We *are* still friends, right?"

I shrugged. "Can't make any promises right now. All I want to do is hibernate. When I wake up, I'll need to make some decisions about where I'm gonna live, in Bayporte or another city. Maybe even move down to the States." Then I slid my arm around Nancy's waist, as warning Bronwen to back off a bit.

It didn't work.

"Ted," Bronwen said, "I'm having a hard time picturing you and your little squeeze here being happy in some trailer park. Do you expect her to cook for you? I'm not sure if that's one of her many talents."

Nancy snarled. "Are you dissin' me, bitch?"

Bronwen didn't even look at Nancy. "Ted, I'm disappointed in you. I didn't know groupies were your thing now."

Nancy said to me, "What did that slut mean about us in a trailer park?"

Nobody said anything for a few minutes. Then Bronwen said to Nancy, "Do you like running around with married men? Is that how you get your kicks?"

Nancy smiled. "Maybe they take up with *me* because their women are inadequate."

Bronwen rolled her eyes at me.

I said, "Maybe we should go get our luggage."

Bronwen said, "Ted, I really do think it would be a good idea if we could talk privately soon."

"No can do," said Nancy.

"I wasn't speaking to *you*," said Bronwen.

"I have your number," I told Bronwen. "I'll call you in the next few days if I get a chance."

"Excuse me?" said Nancy, frowning.

"Relax, Nancy. I have stuff at her place so I have to go there anyway. We're divorced. I am no longer interested in her. A cup of coffee with her while I'm getting my stuff won't do any harm."

Nancy whimpered a bit. "I thought you said you loved me."

"Yes, and I meant it."

"He *didn't* mean it," said Bronwen. "He says things, but he lies. The only person he loves is Teddy C. There's no room for anyone else."

I took Nancy into my arms and gave her a long, hard hug. "All better?" I paused. "But don't be jealous of Bronwen and me. We're divorced but we're still friends. If we see each other from time to time, that's got nothing to do with you and me."

Just then I noticed that we had an audience. A photographer and reporter stood nearby. I asked them who they were and they said they were from *The Bayporter*. They wanted to interview me about my just-ended trip to Europe. I told them I would be happy to give them some time for pictures and questions later on at Troy Frisby's house. Good enough, they said.

"Teddy," the photographer asked me, "would you pose just for one right now? With your wife and sister."

I rolled my eyes at Bronwen and Nancy but they both smirked at the guy's presumptuous remark.

"Teddy tells me you're rich," Nancy said to

Bronwen. "So why do you want him if you can have plenty of other men?"

Bronwen shook her head. "I don't want him the way you do. Been there, done that, I've had better—"

"Enough of that," I told her. "I fucked better than you remember."

She ignored me. "Ted has a good heart. He listens. I have many admirers and acquaintances but few friends. He's one of my true friends." She looked at me and said, "Now, wasn't that a nice thing to say?"

"I'm still smarting over your remark about my sexual prowess."

Nancy sighed and said, "Teddy, let's get out of here *tout de suite*. I'm beat to shit and want to get some sleep."

I nodded. "Let's go. Bronwen, I'll call you soon and we'll talk."

"No you won't," said Nancy. "I'll hide your iPhone."

Nancy and I traipsed over to collect our luggage. I looked over my shoulder and saw Bronwen standing at the statue of the Bayporte Trapper. She was giving him the finger.

Now, as to more current things: I discovered that, while golfing in the Canadian Open at Placid Oaks, if I'm a leader, everyone treats me better.

One evening, Nancy and I went out to dinner with Troy and Andrea. As we sat at our booth, many people came by to say hello and ask *both* of us to pose for pictures. Troy had that sort of stuff happen to him all the time, but not me.

We had driven to a section of Bayporte, near Northup University, filled with chic little boutiques, fancy apartment buildings and palm trees, as if it were trying to become a lookalike for Los Angeles. One of the most popular restaurants in this part of town was Kimo's, a Polynesian joint. When we arrived, dozens of others were standing there, waiting for tables. But the boss hustled us right in and sat us down. The owner, or manager, or whoever he was, smiled as soon as he saw me. He had caught me on the TV news. Then he saw Troy, and that made the man twice as happy.

"Nice that I played good golf today," I said. "We're getting the special treatment."

"Yeah, thank God we have Teddy Crossley with us tonight." Troy snorted. "If it had just been Troy Frisby, we would have waited all night for a table and they would have seated us near the washrooms."

Throughout our meal, people came up to us, timidly or boldly, waving their cell phones. To fit both of you into the picture, you pretty much have to press your faces together, and I didn't like getting that friendly, especially when the person asking for the picture was a guy. Normally I watched Troy do that stuff for a dozen fans at a time and he seemed OK with it, but Troy seldom got bent out of shape in social situations.

"Oh," Troy might say, "and this is my good friend and fellow golfer Teddy Crossley..." and the fan would shrug. Just to be polite, the fan might ask for a picture with me, too, for which he had little desire.

But things were different that night at Kimo's.

"Good golfing, Teddy," says some guy walking past our table, patting me on the shoulder. "Keep doing it right and you're going to win this thing."

Then he sees Troy and says, "Frisby, you keep up the good work too. Nice to see you boys."

Andrea beams at everyone and says, "He's just trying to be polite."

Troy swallows a mouthful of barbecued meat and says, "They can kiss my ass."

Nancy giggles into her napkin.

"It's a weird thing," I say to no one in particular. "Knockin' a puny ball around. One ball, eighteen holes, four or five hours. One goofy shot went into the cup for me but it didn't go in for someone else, so I'm the hero and they're the heel. Jut too weird."

At the conclusion of our meal, the boss insisted on buying us a drink and chatting with us a bit. He solicited some golf advice.

"Always remember the fundamentals," I told him. "Find a good stance, a good swing, a good grip and stay with those things."

"And if that doesn't work," added Troy, "wait till nobody's looking and alter your scorecard."

"Our suppers," Nancy told him, "were delicious. I'm not sure who you hired back there in the kitchen, whether they're Pakis or Chinks or whatever, and I don't know if they're legal to work in Canada, but they can sure cook a good supper."

Back in Troy's guest bedroom, I tried to get up close and personal with Nancy, but she said no. "I've got gas. I've had too many drinks. I can't do it. Sorry."

"I'm not that horny either," I said. "But I'm still bugged about what Bronwen said at the airport: 'Oh, I've had lots better.' Like hell she has. I'm no porno star, but I can get the job done as well as the next man my age."

PART 2:

A TROUBLED CULTURE

HOLE IN ONE

3

On Friday, I suppose for the very first time, I learned firsthand about being a celebrity golfer. The kind of fame that guys like Tiger Woods, Phil Mickelson, Rory McIlroy—and even Troy Frisby— experience all the time.

The only time a golf stud like those guys is safe from the obsessed and admiring hordes is when he's out on the course, hitting the ball. When he's not on the green, he's answering questions about self-evident things, posing for pictures or trying to get out of the clubhouse without having to contend with all those people who, figuratively or literally, want a piece of him.

For reasons I'll never understand, I went out there that day and shot 68, and the day before I shot 70, which made my two-day total 148, and that was better than everyone else's score. I, Teddy Crossley, stood all by myself as the Canadian Open's leader.

Troy played good golf, too; he is incapable of playing bad golf. We walked into the press tent together, sat behind the microphones and teased each other in front of the sportswriters. Troy did his act as King Shit of golf and I played Teddy Nobody. Touring pros love to have an audience to entertain, if only to show that some athletes *do* have charisma.

"Teddy," Troy asked, "which club did you use on the seventh hole?"

I shrugged. "Oh, I guess about a five iron."

"Wow! A five!" Troy winked at our audience. "We'd better get an auditor to check him out, if he's claiming that kind of loft!"

Everyone laughed. Troy's joke was meant for golf insiders. Those who play professionally know that the clubs they use are *not* the same as those normal folks buy at Bob's Golf Shop.

"Troy," I asked, "how did you do on ten?"

"Par," he said.

"Really? I looked over at you and you were so deep into the trees and weeds that I thought you were a vegan fixing your lunch!"

We went back and forth about a few other things. Finally, one of the sportswriters stopped typing on his MacBook Pro and asked us which of us would win.

"Maybe neither of us," Troy said. "It's not just Troy versus Teddy, you know. There are half a dozen guys who could win this thing."

I nodded my concurrence. Glancing up at the leader board, I felt the most intense and immense gratification at seeing my name at the top, although I wasn't quite dumb enough to think it would stay up there for the rest of the tournament. Still…

T. Crossley………..70-68   138

T. Frisby………….71-69   140

P. Mickelson……... 72-71 143

R. McIlroy……….. 72-72 144

T. Woods…………72-70   142

"Tiger," I said to the sports reporters. "He's only four shots back. He could very easily win this thing. I'd be worried about him even if he came out just with a putter."

"Teddy," a reporter asked, "if it came down to it at

the end of this weekend, you and Troy Frisby would be paired together. Would you be OK with that?"

"Oh, that would be fine," I replied. "Troy and I have been friends for years, and I've played so many rounds with him already that I would completely relaxed."

"And this tournament wouldn't have any impact on your friendship?" asked the reporter.

Troy said, "You *always* want to have some friends at these tournaments, even though you know that one guy is going to win and the others aren't. I would much rather play against a bunch of guys I know than a bunch of strangers." Then, "I don't know if you guys know this, but Teddy has never won a major, so I'm hoping that if I don't win this one, he will. And I'm sure he's hoping that if he doesn't win, I will."

"No," I said. "I want Tiger to win if I don't. In case you guys didn't hear, he got divorced and now he has to pay alimony and child support."

Everybody had a nice big laugh, and Troy said, "Teddy's catching on fast, isn't he? I've been coaching him on how to perform for the media."

After we were done with the media, or they were done with us—I had a hard time figuring out whose idea it was to terminate the session—Troy went off to hit some balls and some men in suits from the TV network invited me to the clubhouse where some *Canadian Sports* writers and editors wanted to chat me up over drinks. Their invitation thrilled me because those guys usually drank and talked with Tiger Woods, Phil Mickelson and Mark O'Meara, or maybe Troy Frisby. They cared little about Teddy Nobody.

It's all kinds of fun to hang out with the men in suits from New York and Toronto from the TV networks and big-time magazines. The food and liquor are premium and the fans don't bug you to pose for pictures because they're too intimidated by the suits.

I didn't lie to myself that I had become the Next Big Thing in golf. I knew that the suits wanted to know about me just in case, by some huge fluke, I won this tournament. If that happened, and I instantly became the sport's newest darling, they wanted to instantly answer the expected question, "Who *is* this guy and how come he just won this tournament?"

"Well," I told the suits, "so far in my mediocre little golfing career I haven't won anything worth bragging about, and I haven't won this thing yet even though I seem to be pretty much in control. But big-time golf is full of guys who blow it in major ways when the pressure mounts, so don't call me the winner until I've actually *won* the bloody thing."

I added that I certainly didn't want to bad-mouth *Canadian Sports* magazine, especially since I read it from cover to cover each month in fifteen minutes— which is easy because it's mostly just advertising—but its editors had to admit something: they had a habit of interviewing probable winners in various sports, gushing all over them and convincing them that they had already won.

"In golf," I explained, "you don't win because of your best efforts. You win *despite* your best efforts. Golf is never about winning the most; it's about losing the least. Each golfer is God's lonely man, and he has enemies all around him. We golfers smile and shake hands and pretend we're friends, but we actually wish each other the worst. And, of course, each golfer's biggest enemy is himself."

One of the suits asked me if I was starting to feel the pressure of playing in a big tournament *and* playing in front of my hometown fans.

I shook my head. "I'm keeping busy just trying to stay focused and make quality shots. I'm treating this like just another tournament, even though it's obviously not that." Then, "When I remember that Tiger Woods and Phil Mickelson and Troy Frisby are also right behind me on the board, I can't really take the idea too seriously that I might *win* this thing. Those guys are relentless competitors who do their best work when they absolutely *must*, but if when Sunday comes and I'm still at the top or close to it. I'm used to pressure from when I played at Beaver Hills. I was just a kid, and I used to bet twenty-five bucks when I only had ten in my pocket."

I believe that if you are a gambler, you don't take money that seriously and you secretly laugh at people who take money *too* seriously. Many of my competitors at Placid Oaks were so hungry for that big payday that they might choke, even if they didn't necessarily need the check.

Me, I've never cared that much about money except when I needed it for a specific reason. But I've seen a hundred rich guys almost have panic attacks because they've had to sell off an asset or two, or part with the interest payment they've just received, because an unexpected expense just came up.

I couldn't imagine having so much money that I would worry about how to hide, or protect, my money from the government, and *then* worrying about how much the lawyers and accountants would charge to help me hide that loot. But I've met my share of men who did exactly that.

During my marriage to Helga Wark, a woman who could burn through money faster than anyone I'd ever met, I started hiding cash around the house so she couldn't spend it, and I even made regular deposits into my bank account. Her idea of domestic responsibility was making sure that both our sports cars had full gas tanks.

She found some of my cash under my computer keyboard as she went online in search of a cure for an STD.

She shook the wad in my face.

"Holding out on me, eh?"

"You're amazing," I said. "You come up with the disease, you give it to me, then you accuse *me* of mistreating *you*."

"I'm sorry about that, but I think the disease came from those dirty glasses or plates from Paul's Sub Stop. I don't think Paul cleans things enough."

I shook my head. "It's gonorrhea. You get it from hoochie-coo, not glasses and plates."

"Who says?"

"The experts. The ones who know."

"The experts lie," she said.

"Kinda doubt that. I think you were getting very friendly with the wrong people. They gave you the gift that keeps on giving."

Helga pouted. "I have friends.. We hang out. They're just guys like you."

"Except that they have STDs and I don't."

She harrumphed. "I still say I got it from a restaurant or washroom or something."

"Kinda doubt that," I repeated.

"The doctors and scientists don't know *everything*,"

she said. "They get things wrong all the time, and this is one of those times. You'll see. Time will prove me right and them wrong."

"Helga," I said, quickly losing my patience. "It's an STD. You can't get it except by boning."

She started whimpering.

I added, "I can go to a doctor and get it checked out. I just wish you could do your pastimes with a vacant vagina."

Helga whimpered some more. "I don't want you to think I'm a slut, sweetie. It's just that I get so lonely. I'm sure there are pastimes other than goonin' and diddlin' and whatever, but I haven't really looked into it. I like to watch movies, too, so maybe I should do that more often.

"You know, the other day I got so pissed on Canadian Comfort and Mountain Dew while you were out golfing in another city, and my friend Dale came by with some pot. We got fucked up and watched some porn videos. Plus, he gave me some money to spend on myself."

"You took money for sex?" I asked her. "That kinda makes you a hooker, hey?"

"Well," she said, sounding indignant, "I wasn't about to screw him for free. Anyway, I don't like Dale Easley that much."

"Helga, you're one of the prettiest girls I know, but if you keep putting out like this, you're going to become the laughingstock of Bayporte. Is that what you want?"

She frowned. "I could go on the road with you, but I really hate those golf matches. All that standing around with nothing to do unless you're a golfer. But don't you think Tiger Woods has a great ass? Do you think he would boff me?"

"Why don't you get a respectable job? Start a new career?"

"They tell me I could make a pile of money if I became a really exclusive call girl. Maybe they have a point. I could never understand why girls spread their legs for free. We should all charge our men for sex, because we have what they want."

"I can't argue with that. If you want to sell sex, just make sure you don't get busted."

Helga sighed and shook her head. "Why does life have to be full of so many difficult decisions? Why can't we all just get along and respect each other's dignity?"

"Well," I said, "if you ever discover the answer to those questions, be sure and tell me."

Helga narrowed her eyes. "Start a career? I don't know what I would do. The only thing I've ever been good for is lovin'."

The subject of money always makes me think about Helga's brothers and their attempt at making big bucks fast when we were teenagers.

Willy and Robby Wark decided to become car thieves. They saw a reality-based TV show and concluded that those with the brains, brawn and balls to steal vehicles and drive them to chop shops could score easy, big money. During this time, some of us jocks crashed a sorority meeting at Rhoda Goldman's house. Back then, jocks liked to attend sorority meetings, and sorority sisters liked having the boys there. Or, if the girls didn't like it, they knew better than to speak up.

We would wait outside while the sorority girls made their young pledges describe their sexual experiences in such detail that the pledges often went red-faced and wept.

Then we would show up, devour their food and strut around in our Northup University jock jackets while the older girls figured out which of them would do which of us.

We always enjoyed going to Rhoda Goldman's big fine house. They had zillions of dollars and enough food to feed the entire neighborhood. We also liked Rhoda because she had great boobs.

Willy Wark had gone out with Rhoda until he figured out she wasn't his kind.

'Rhoda's a kike,' he said. 'Who woulda guessed?'

'Her name is Goldman,' I said. 'Didn't you know that she's Jewish?'

'Bruce Springsteen's got a kike name,' Willy said, 'but he's Catholic or somethin'.'

Willy and Robby left Rhoda's that day with several small items they took to Faith's Auction House and sold for $200.

At night, the Wark boys dressed in black and went out to steal Hondas, Fords and Nissans. They drove those cars a dozen blocks through rainy, empty streets and disappeared into dark garages, where their connections paid them in cash. Soon they wanted better cars and more money.

They decided to steal the Goldmans' Mercedes.

Willy, Robby and I had spent a couple of hours nibbling on Nachos and drinking beer at Paul's Submarine Stop. We decided to drive over to Rhoda's house, eat a substantial meal, listen to some music and ogle her breasts.

So we did. We sat with her on her sofa and told dirty jokes. Her mother fixed us a platter of sandwiches, which he all found delicious but insufficient. Willy and Robby snarled and staggered into the kitchen.

"Do not be alarmed,' I overhead Willy saying. "But we have to seize your Mercedes because you are kikes and we're neo-Nazis. Give me the keys."

Mrs. Goldman said, "Not funny, Willy."

Willy bolted outside to try jimmying open the car's door. Robby got Mrs. Goldman into a chokehold and said, "You ever heard of the Holocaust?"

"Robby," I said, "this is bullshit. Stop trying to kill Rhoda's mum."

Willy came in wiping his brow. "That's the best car I've seen yet. It should be worth a few bucks, hey?"

Rhoda shook her head. "You can't be serious."

"But I can't get past the lock to get inside the car," Willy said. "These new cars are tricky buggers. I think I'll need the key."

Mrs. Goldman, who was just getting her wind back after Robby freed her from his chokehold, took a few deep breaths. "If you don't leave now, I'll call the police and press charges."

"This is not funny, you guys," said Rhoda.

Robby and Willy smirked at each other. "Give us the keys," Robby said to Mrs. Goldman.

"Never," she said. "Get out, you filthy pigs."

"I know what we'll do," said Robby. He grabbed a hank of Mrs. Goldman's hair and pulled her across the room, then flung her into the pantry and locked the door.

Do something! Rhoda mouthed at me.

I just stared at her, unsure of how to stop the Warks. I'd had enough experience with them to know that the best thing was just to let them have their fun until they grew bored and wandered off. They got bored faster when they were drunk, as they were now. Rhoda started looking around for a knife, but Willy came up to her and started staring at her breasts.

"Don't be mean," she said. "Remember, it's just me, Rhoda."

Willy nodded. "Yeah, and I'm Willy, and there's Robby and Teddy, and your mum's locked in the pantry."

We all stood and listened as Mrs. Goldman pounded on the door and shrieked.

"You should let her out," I said.

"How come?" asked Willy. "She's got tons of food in there if she gets hungry."

"Wark boys gone wild," I muttered.

"Teddy," Robby said, "we're having fun. You don't have to join in, but I know you like fun."

"Sick bastards," said Rhoda. "Get out of my house."

I nodded. "Time to leave. Rhoda, lovely to see you again. Thank your mum for those delicious sandwiches."

"Robby!" shouted Willy. "Their fuckin' car won't start without the keys!"

"Shitfuck," replied Robby. "The best cars are the hardest to steal. We'll leave it for later." He searched through the refrigerator until he found a handful of tomatoes. "These'll have to do."

Willy threw Rhoda over his shoulder as the two boys marched into the living room. After giving her ass a hard slap, he dropped her on the sofa.

Robby did a pitcher's windup and fired a tomato at one of the paintings on the wall. The red orb splattered all over the artwork.

"Robby," I said, "knock that shit off. Those paintings could be worth a million dollars."

Robby replied, "Watch your smart bloody mouth, Teddy. Whose side are you on, anyway? The kikes or the Canadians?"

Rhoda lay cowering on the sofa. Willy said, "I wanna see your rack," and made her hold up her arms as he yanked off her sweatshirt and brassiere. "Wanna see your junk, too," he added, pulling off her Levi's and undies.

"What are you guys gonna do next?" I asked. "So far, it's assault and vandalism. Wanna try for rape and murder? You know what they do to boys like you in prison?"

"We won't get busted," Robby said, firing another tomato at a painting. "Nobody's gonna tell on us. Right, Rhoda? Nobody's gonna say nothin'. We're gonna pretend that this never happened, because if we get into trouble, we got two brothers at home who will come by to finish the job."

Rhoda lay in the fetal position, whimpering.

"Well," I said, "you guys won't kill *me* because I'm a jock and your friend. What would you do without me?"

Robby frowned and nodded. A dead Teddy would be more bad than good.

"Come on, boys," I said. "You've scared these nice ladies enough already. Rhoda, you can put your clothes back on. We're gonna go rob a gas station or something."

"I wanna drop a deuce," Robby said.

"Washroom's down the hallway," Rhoda said.

"No, I wanna do it here," he said.

"Don't you fucking dare," Rhoda said, glowering.

He dropped his pants and squatted but could not perform the function. Then we left.

I saw very little of Rhoda after that evening. I heard that she withdrew from Northup. I found it odd that she had studied there, because Bayporte's wealthier families usually sent their kids to American or European colleges. Unless, of course, those kids really wanted to stay close to home, which they rarely did. I read that her father, the owner of ritzy, exclusive Goldman's Jewelers, had sold his store, although the new owners kept its name.

Willy and Robby, still believing in their original business plan, went home and tried to steal their father's pickup truck, take it to the chop shop and report it to the police as stolen.

Their father went ballistic when he saw what they were up to. He punched their faces and kicked their scrotums. Either Wark brother could have taken their father in two minutes if it came down to a fight, but they considered hitting him disrespectful.

The old man made them go out into the backyard and beat each other senseless as he drank down several bottles of Diefenbaker beer. At the conclusion of their fight, as the two boys lay on their backs, bloodied and battered, their father pulled out his pecker and urinated in their faces as they lay on their backs, struggling to breathe.

I hoped that the boys had finally gotten adequate punishment. But no; that thrashing only made them more determined not to get caught in the future. Also, the Warks weren't always up to no good. Some of their hijinks were just ways for them to cope with the *ennui* of being youngsters in Bayporte, the rainiest, dreariest city in the universe.

The Warks, like all the other Gentiles I knew, hated Jews, and their bad feelings extended to Catholics, although I didn't think they could recognize one if they went to the Vatican.

Willy once said, "Jesus was a Christian. I don't know how he could stand to be around all them kikes."

The Warks knew of a local costume store that stocked priests' apparel. They loved to rent vestments and pretend to be drunk as people exited from shopping malls or movie theaters.

One time, a nice man saw Robby's collar and said, "Pardon me, Father, but you seem to be in some distress. May I help you?"

Robby, lisping like a Fag City sissy, replied, "Well, the Pope just had me fired for buggering too many altar boys. I'm feeling very lonely. Could we go someplace private and talk about it?"

The man backed off, unable to figure out if he'd just been made the butt of a practical joke, then he hurried away. The Wark brothers doubled over in hilarity and passed around their bottle of Canadian Comfort. They did a terrific acting job as five muscular priests, especially when one didn't look closely enough at their faces to see the striking Wark family resemblance. While guzzling Canadian Comfort and shouting obscenities at passersby, the boys would smack each other's ass and grab each other's balls.

Willy, wearing his fake collar, once yelled at a horde of moviegoers standing in line for tickets, "If you go to Rome and see an old man dressed all in white, tell him I'm having fun here in Bayporte screwing everything I can!"

Since everyone in the queue had a cell phone, somebody called the police. When the cruiser arrived, the cops laughed at the Warks' getup. One cop said,

"As soon as they told me what was going on, I thought, 'That sounds like those bloody Wark boys having a bit of fun.' So, Willy, how are your mum and dad, eh?'"

The Warks went to plenty of trouble when they played their best-ever joke, which was on Helga and me when we decided to get married. They came to get me at Beaver Hill and stuck a knife under my chin. "We're taking you to a bachelor party," Willy Wark told me. They drove me downtown, to the lobby pub at the Pattison Hotel, and made me drink beer until I could neither walk nor talk. Then they carried me to the tattoo parlor next door, where I passed out. When I woke up, hung over and bleary eyed, I discovered a fresh tat on my left buttock saying that I was the property of Helga Wark. I also noted that they had misspelled their own name.

Becoming a touring professional golfer taught me, if nothing else, that I ought to choose my friends with a bit more care than I usually had. Back at Beaver Hills, I had fallen into polite conversations with virtually all who cared to speak to me, even if I didn't especially care for the look or sound of those people.

I'm not sure if my friendship with Troy Frisby was good or bad. But I did learn plenty about certain aspects of the golfer's life by spending so much time with him.

Troy, despite his fine manners and charisma, is a considerable egotist and snob, and I followed his lead, figuratively speaking, as we hung out together. From him I figured out what to pack in my suitcases, which tournaments weren't worth my time and effort, which hotels and restaurants were good and bad, which people to know, which ones to avoid. In other words, who was cool and who was a goof.

When a person is in a new milieu, he assumes that everyone he encounters who acts important is just that. Most of them are fakers, and the neophyte learns this by how quickly the faker is willing to accept the newcomer and introduce him to the other fakers.

During my very first month on the tour I played with Troy one day in southern California when some local guy with a blazer started going on about some competition he had played in with Fuzzy Zoeller, the world-class golfer who had been shamed into retirement by publicly making fun of Tiger Woods. "So then Fuzzy said—"

Troy smiled at him and said, "Look, guy, if this is going to be a long story, tell us later on—like after we've left town."

It's probably a bad idea to be rude to these people who go to so much trouble organizing tournaments for people like Troy and me. They are full-time members of the clubs that host these events, and they are quite gracious when they see us come to town.

But, as Troy pointed out, "I'll be damned if I'll just stand there all day and let the bloody guy talk my ear off."

You go along to get along, I guess.

One time, at Sundown Country Club in the Great Elizabeth interior a couple of hours from Bayporte, a fancy gentleman wearing a committeeman's blazer gave Troy the eye while asking him about why Troy won the purse so easily. "You were just *marvelous*, Troy. I just couldn't *believe* how well you swung your club today."

Troy thanked the man for his kind words.

"What are you doing this evening?" the man asked.

Troy looked at me and patted his pocket. "My cell phone is vibrating."

"Probably your wife," I said. "Important call. You should take it now."

So we took off, leaving that fancy gentleman to wonder who he would hang out with that evening. In my MacBook Pro and iPhone, I now have a long list of people to avoid throughout North America and beyond. Those people mean well, but they bore the shit out of me with their nonstop talk about their new Pings or the can't-lose financial deals they could get me in on.

Their wives, too, were pains in my ass. If they got tipsy, they might threaten to make a scene if I refused to dance with them to some Michael Jackson ballad. Or maybe they would be Internet-junkie teetotalers who insisted on telling me what they had learned about Warren Beatty and Annette Bening's firstborn who had recently gone tranny, or Ally Sheedy's lesbian teenaged daughter.

Troy Frisby indulged the wives if they were moderately pretty. Troy, a lifelong cocksman, said that a woman's age made little difference to him.

"How," I once asked him, "can you get turned on by those country-club hens who just gossip and brag all the time?"

"They're lonely and I'm virile," he said. "I provide a public service." Troy thrived on challenges, on and off the golf course. When he met a golf wife who aroused him sufficiently, he would make friends with her family and invite them to come watch him play. Sometimes he even managed to get Tiger Woods to come over and say hi to the speechless family whose matriarch Troy was trying to *shtup*. Or Troy might offer free golf lessons to the woman's spoiled-rotten adolescent children.

By and by they would come to view the famous, handsome Troy Frisby as a personal friend, and even a nominal family member.

He would have to work for what he wanted, of course, and it might take a year or more, but he *would* get into her pants.

"Those women can't be worth all that trouble," I once said to him.

"Oh, but they *are*," he replied. "I'm giving them

what they didn't even know they wanted. They're grateful and gratified."

Often, he gets them with much less effort. In places such as southern California and Florida, golf wives can be hotter than July. *They* do the seducing. They don't waste their time, and they try not to waste yours. You can get laid between breakfast and brunch, and that applies to all of us, not just Troy Frisby.

At most of the big tournaments, the facilities for everything are arranged to make screwing around very convenient, as if the people who had designed the hotels, restaurants, bars and golf courses knew how much hanky-panky would be happening. The logistics had to be right for those liaisons.

Troy had fun slipping back to his room with this or that mature woman whose husband was delighted to be in Pebble Beach, or Augusta, or wherever else, sharing a golf course with the best of the best.

"Why do those women mess around like that?" I asked.

"Because," he said, "once they have lots of money and their kids are married or in college, they get bored."

Troy got media attention by growing his hair to his shoulders, then cutting it short. He grew a beard, replaced it with a goatee, then got rid of that, too. A dapper clotheshorse, he wore Brioni and Versace casual outfits on the course, which hardly helped his game but got him lots of attention. He bought his attire on Rodeo Drive in Beverly Hills and at Wilkes Bashford in San Francisco. Americans, listening to his tongue-in-cheek answers during interviews, giggled at his Canadian accent, and sports magazines called him the snazziest golfer around. Troy's image keeps his public interested in him. His golfing abilities are inconsistent.

"When I'm on that course," he told me, "whether I'm playing well or not, I want people to point and say, 'There he is! There's Troy! Check him out!'"

Troy, a world-class cocksman, wants to attain goals comparable to those of the late porn superstar John C. Holmes. He wanted to fornicate on a commercial aircraft. I know he did it because I saw him, sort of. He got a flight attendant to enter a lavatory with him. Fifteen minutes later—I timed them—they reemerged, and Troy winked at me.

Much later, he told me that, for a stud like himself, he needed to make things a bit more difficult. He wanted to do it in first class, not during the in-flight movie and not in some isolated part of the aircraft. Finally, he had to do it while his missus was also on board.

"Good luck with that," I said.

Troy told me that he did it on the half-empty, Honolulu-to-Bayporte run as the aircraft darkened in the late-afternoon sky. In the upstairs lounge, he met a woman who followed golf and she kept touching his arm as she spoke to him.

Troy poured Chardonnay down Andrea's gullet till she nodded out, then he moved down a few rows to be with his new friend. He covered them both with a blanket and went to town.

"I'll never forget what's-her-name," he said with a small sigh.

He once explained to me why women seemed to like him so much, though I had not asked him about it and did not especially wish to hear his views. He spoke to me as if I were a pimply, adolescent onanist desperately in need of his guidance.

"I am a handsome man," he said. "You think I don't know this? I also look a bit decadent and dissolute, as if I've already had too much of the good life. I always look them in the eye and tell them whatever bullshit they want to hear."

"That makes sense," I replied. "But I've seen you chat up one chick while you checked out someone else. If I were a chick, I would resent it."

"Well, maybe she's checking out other guys while I'm checking her out. You see, Ted, the idea is to project complete sincerity. When a cocksman can fake that, the seductions become easy. I could have been an actor, and in many ways I am. I'm putting on performances all the time."

"Maybe, after you retire from golf, you'll go to Hollywood and get some screen work."

"I hope to do just that. Anyway, a good seducer," he went on, "needs to be patient. I knew this one woman in San Francisco? She was a stripper but very beautiful. It took me two years to get her into the sack, but when it happened? *Blam! Zoom!*"

"That good, eh?" I said.

"Finally," he said, "preparation is crucial. Be ready

to perform. Forget that Viagra nonsense. Show up with a natural, drug-free boner. You'll be glad you did."

I nodded.

Troy Frisby, I thought, should have been born into a rich southern California family. Deep down inside—to the extent that he *has* a deep down inside—he is a spoiled brat.

"Teddy," he has said, "in this world, there are the haves and have-nots. The have-nots want to screw you over, so you have to screw *them* over first. People want me to fuck up because I'm tall, blond, handsome, rich and successful, and they're not. Well, fuck *them*, too."

Troy, if he saw a drowning man, might throw the guy a rope if it didn't put him to excessive inconvenience. He is far too much like the overprivileged Californians I have met.

I have concluded that the Golden State's Republicans have implemented instruction in callousness as part of their schools' curriculum. California, I think, has the best bad and good things in America, so why are they so stingy with their goodies?

Troy grew up in the ritzy part of Toronto. His family had money. He had looks, talent, charisma. His sisters were knockouts. He chose his friends and acquaintances with the utmost care.

"Troy is an asshole," said Bronwen. "He thinks people should be thrown in jail if they can't swim, ride a bike or maintain a year-round suntan."

Throughout our friendship, I had watched Troy tip bartenders, servers, taxi drivers, and even caddies, with chump change.

"What's up with that?" I asked him. "Don't they deserve more? They have to make a living, too."

"Who cares? If they want to make decent money, let them get off their lazy asses and find decent jobs."

"How much," I asked him, "would you pay a really good caddy who helped you choose clubs and make good shots?"

Troy laughed. "Well, if I needed a *caddy's* advice on how to do *my* job, I shouldn't be a pro golfer. I would be an accountant or something."

"I find your empathy very moving."

"Teddy," he said, "you can't go out there and play

golf, or baseball, or any other sport, and think, 'Well, my competitor is down on his luck and he's such a nice guy, I think I'll let him win.' If that's your attitude, you should go back to school and become a priest or social worker. In order to be a winner, you have to make sure the other guy is a loser."

I shook my head. "You sound so damn greedy. In the golf tour, there's one fat purse after another. There are enough goodies to go around."

"No," he said. "I want it all. I absolutely want it all." Then, "But I can never have it all. Whenever I get mine, I have to give half to the tax man so he can give it to the welfare cases."

"You amaze me," I told him. "You have a fancy house, a pretty wife and lots of cute girlfriends. You also have a moderate amount of fame and you like your job most of the time. We have a troubled culture because of guys like you."

Troy frowned. "What does my wife have to do with my girlfriends? Andrea is a trophy. I won her at some tournament."

"She's not a trophy. She is your wife. You love her, don't you?"

"Yes," he said. "I also love making a hole in one. I've done that twice, several years ago, and can remember both of them as clearly as yesterday. *That's* love. Women are like buses. They come and go every fifteen minutes."

"Shit."

Troy looked off into the distance. "A hole in one. Two times it's happened. It may never happen again. That's the bitch of it."

"So," I said, "you're saying that in order to become a successful competitor, you have to be a ruthless, heartless son of a bitch. Is that about right?"

"I'm a golfer," Troy said. "I have no teammates to hit a home run if I strike out. If I fuck up, I have only myself to blame. The day I let people push me around and mess with my head, I'm finished. I need to be able to say, 'Fuck everybody and everyone, I'm here to play golf,' and *mean* it."

"In the grand scheme of things," I asked him, "do you really think yours is the best outlook?"

Troy smirked. "In the grand scheme of things, nobody exists."

4

When a new guy begins the tournament, and he has a formidable reputation from being an amateur, many other golfers, especially Troy Frisby, want to see him fail. The newcomer, you understand, may be a huge threat to our livelihoods.

They emotionally traumatized the new stud, Harold Baumer.

Harold began his professional career with a fine stroke and a surfeit of confidence. He had won every amateur competition of significance.

A tall, rangy, affable man, Harold made the PGA circuit after missing the cut a bunch of times. But the sports magazines still wrote about him as one of those "PGA superstars who didn't happen."

When I first met him, Harold had to be the most naturally talented golfer I had seen in a long while. He had swept most of the prestigious amateur competitions, which impressed me a great deal. But Harold, the most *gullible* human alive, naively listened to crafty, manipulative assholes like Troy Frisby.

"Harold," I said, "don't listen to these knuckleheads. They don't have your best interests in mind."

"But Troy said—"

"What Troy said don't mean shit around here. If he told you to hit your ball into the Tyson River, would you do it?"

Harold frowned and rubbed his chin. "Troy told me to stop wearing gloves and change my grip. He wants me to eat more breakfast and less lunch, or vice versa. He thinks I should wear darker or lighter clothing—I can't remember which."

I nodded. "He probably also wants you to putt with your eyes closed."

"He didn't say anything about that."

"Troy wants you to fix everything that ain't broke."

Harold, like a medical student whose mental tumblers simply will not stop, would sit like a zombie at dinner, eating his food and frowning as he sorted through the bogus advice people had given him that day.

In Deep South tournament once, I stepped out for a short walk and a breath of fresh air and discovered Harold teeing up and whacking balls at midnight.

"What the hell," I asked, "are you doing?"

"Troy told me to practice at night. There are fewer distractions."

I rolled my eyes. "The only time you should listen to him is when he's talking about sex, and even then he's usually full of shit."

Harold would sometimes think he had discovered the secrets to playing great golf after he had finished the day in the top five or ten, but then he would psyche himself and leave town with empty pockets. He would shoot a magnificent round occasionally, just to remind everyone of his capacities. He went halfway through one tournament with a score in the low 60s, but lost his composure and did a high 80s. He then packed up and drove off to the next competition.

"Teddy," he once asked me, "when you're making

an easy putt, do you ever imagine that the cup is as big as a swimming pool?"

"Can't say as I do," I replied.

"Do you ever think that the cup has magical powers?"

"Fuck no."

"Have you ever stood out there and thought you might be wearing the wrong clothes?" he asked.

"You mean, do I ever play golf in my wife's clothes?"

"Have you ever prepared to make a six-inch putt and wondered if God Almighty Himself was watching you? That maybe He was deciding whether or not to let you sink that putt?"

I just looked away.

"Teddy," he continued, "I had a puny little putt to make once, but I kept thinking that He was displeased with me and that I didn't deserve to make that putt. Do you want to know what happened?"

I certainly didn't. "Do tell."

"Well, instead of tapping the ball into the cup, I started hitting myself with the putter. People said they could hear me saying, 'Sinner, sinner, sinner!'"

"Did you sink that puny putt?" I asked.

He shook his head. "I dropped out instead."

Wherever and whenever he plays, Harold has a childlike ebullience that makes him popular with fans. Still, if you were to ask him, I'm sure he would say that I'm his best friend, although I'm not sure what we have in common besides golf and alternative music fans. He once said that I had taught him a great deal, though I'm not sure what.

After graduating from the University of Nevada at Las Vegas with a number of amateur victories to brag about, Harold started hanging out with me while I was hanging out with Troy.

"Why do you bring him along?" Troy asked. "He's ugly. The chicks don't like him."

"He respects your abilities as a golfer," I replied. "He means no harm. He's just trying to make friends."

Troy snarled. "I have too many friends already. People on Facebook are bugging me all the time with friend requests. This guy Harold? He keeps inviting women to visit him in Las Vegas while I'm trying to seduce them. Next time, I'm just going to tell him to fuck off."

"Well," I said, "he's *my* friend. If he seems lonely and could use some fun, I'm going to invite him along with us."

Troy, a world-class opportunist, saw an ideal way of exploiting single, eager-to-please Harold, who wanted Troy's approval. Troy decided to use Harold to get laid.

Many times, when Andrea insisted on traveling with Troy, one of his old girlfriends would materialize to be Harold's date. The six of us would go out to dinner: Andrea and Troy, Nancy and me, Harold and Troy's girlfriend.

At a tournament in the Southeast, Troy talked one of his honeys, Jessie, into driving out to have dinner with us, ostensibly as Harold's date.

"We'll go somewhere dark and cozy," Troy confided to me, "so that Jessie and I can play kneesies or footsies under the table or maybe even sneak off for a quickie."

He chose the Seven Seas, a trendy joint with a

puny dance floor and a deafening sound system. The food was stale, the service slow and the prices high. Troy didn't care; the item he wanted to eat did not appear on the menu.

Jessie had long dark hair, a deep tan, miles of legs and a "don't you wish you were me?" attitude. I bet she was wanted in a dozen states for breaking hearts.

Troy knew someone who knew someone at the restaurant. They sat us outside, scarcely an improvement over the inside. We sat in the stifling, brackish air and tried to talk to each other above the *thump-bump-pump* of dance music. Then we smartened up a bit and started mouthing our words. Too bad we didn't know sign language

How's work going? Troy asked Jessie, mute. *Like your job?*

Work's OK, she said. *I got divorced, and that changed things.*

I caught Troy's eye and said, *When's your next tournament?*

He shook his head. No golf talk tonight.

Presently the music ended.

"Maybe," said Troy in his normal voice, "we

125

should go somewhere else. Someplace quieter."

"No," said Jessie. "This area has boomed. All the nightclubs are this loud."

Harold asked, "Why can't we just stay here for a while?"

"I'm sitting in the wrong place. I'm too close to the music," said Troy. "OK if I move to the other end of the table?"

Harold nodded. "Good idea. Jessie and I are gonna get up and dance in a few minutes."

Troy nodded and lit up a Player's Light. I caught our server's eye and gestured that we wanted another round of cocktails.

Troy said, "Jessie, how long have you lived in the Southeast?"

"She's been here—" said Harold.

"Thank you, Harold, but I was speaking to Jessie."

Jessie chuckled. "Going on five years. I moved down here from Oberlin, Ohio. I'm working now as an assistant manager at the Southern Bell, with no *e*."

Harold nodded. "Troy, we've been there, right?"

Troy shrugged. "I've been to so many places, I don't remember them all."

Jessie's eyes narrowed a bit. "The Southern Bell. Good food, not exactly cheap. Good ambiance. Popular with young couples and families with money."

"Sounds fun," said Andrea. "Maybe Troy and I should go there."

Harold nodded. "Yeah, I've been there. Lots of cute young things just hanging out. Right, Troy?"

Troy stood up and headed to the men's room.

Jessie stood up and headed to the ladies' room.

Within ten minutes, Troy returned, alone.

Harold got up and started looking for Jessie. Presently he came back, frowning and hangdog, and told us that he caught up with her as she got into a taxi.

"She told me she had gotten an urgent call on her cell phone from her uncle or cousin, who had just gotten into town and needed to see her. She said to tell you guys that she enjoyed seeing us and that we all need to get together again real soon."

The dance music started up again, even louder, and Troy looked through his cell phone messages, as he often did when bored shitless and wanting to go home.

I mouthed to him, *I guess Jessie's uncle made her a better offer.*

Back at Placid Oaks, Harold could do nothing right. His shots almost invariably ended up in the water or in the rough. He finished with an abysmal 82.

He needed to play much better to make the cut, and most of the time, he was capable of doing just that. I thought he might finish at under 70, and so did he, but then his demons took over and he couldn't hit anything straight. He missed the cut by one stroke.

After having cocktails with the suits from back east, I loitered in the locker room with Troy. Harold soon came in and collapsed onto one of the plastic chairs. He blew out a huge breath.

"I can't cope with sand traps," he said. "I can get out of the rough easily enough, but those sand traps? They just kick my ass every time."

Troy and I sat on one of the benches. Some of the other golfers had stopped in for a few minutes, then left. A few sports reporters had come by, too.

"Everybody," I said, "hates sand traps."

"You guys played OK, I noticed," Harold said.

"I was brilliant," I said.

"Like hell," Troy said. "You were struggling, just like the rest of us. I watched you."

"We really have to get our shit together," Harold said. "This course is one tough son of a bitch. Are all the Canadian courses this hard?"

"Oh, this one gets harder as you go along," I told him.

"Maybe," said Harold, "I need a new set of clubs. I'll go to Nike and say, 'Give me whatever you're giving Tiger.'"

"Harold," I said, "you don't need a new set of clubs. You just need to relax, take it easy and enjoy yourself."

"I need a new putter. All great golfers are great putters," he said.

"Except Troy Frisby." I smirked.

"Sad but true," Troy said. "My mediocre putting is my great weakness."

"You often make the putts that really count," I reminded him.

"But not often enough," he retorted.

"Me neither," said Harold. "I need to try a different putter. Troy, do you have an old one you would lend me?"

"Nope."

"Why the hell not?"

"Because," said Troy, "I need all my clubs at my disposal at all times."

"Then what should I do?" Harold threw up his hands.

"Maybe go to a pro shop and *buy* a new putter?" Troy suggested.

"Come on, Troy," I said. "Let him borrow your old Titleist putter. You know that new putters are as useless as new shoes. You have to break them in before they're any good."

"No can do," said Troy.

"Why not?" I asked. "Harold here just missed the cut, and he asked you to lend him your putter, but you say no. He's supposed to be your friend. Why are you being such an asshole?"

"Forget it," Harold said. "I'll borrow someone else's putter."

"Maybe," I said, "it's not your putter. It could be

your behavior. You get all jittery and start twitching sometimes. You need to be cool, calm and collected."

Troy said, "Take away Tiger's custom-made Nike clubs and I wonder how many majors he'd win."

"Tiger doesn't make every putt," Harold said. "He's a much better overall player than he is a putter, if you ask me."

"I've seen him play many times when his short game wasn't going so great," Troy said. "I've made shots Tiger could only fantasize about."

"Oh?" I arched an eyebrow. "I suppose all those green jackets he's won were just flukes?"

"Tiger plays well under pressure," Troy conceded. "He has cool. But don't tell me that he's King Shit of golf. There are many quality players out here."

"If golf were a team sport," I told him, "I'd sure as hell want him on *my* side."

"Shit," Harold said. "One of you guys might win this thing. I might just cancel my travel plans and stay here to see how this tournament ends."

"Dammit, Harold!" Troy pointed a finger at him. "You're too much of a fan and not enough of a player. You can't be a successful competitor if you're in awe of the other golfers."

"I just don't feel like a winner right now. If I went off to the next tournament," Harold said, "I'd fail to make the cut there and would just sit in my hotel room and watch this Open on TV. At least here I can watch it in person and cheer for you two."

"Wrong attitude," Troy said. "As soon as you missed the cut here, you should have packed up and gone to the next tournament. Don't cheer for anyone and don't expect anyone to cheer for you. Simple as that."

"But you are my friends, and this is the Canadian Open, a big deal. If you win this thing, I want to be here to congratulate you," Harold told us.

I smiled. "That's very touching, Harold. I'm keeping my fingers crossed that I can keep playing this well so that Troy here doesn't end up winning. He'll just wave the trophy in our faces and tell us to suck his cock."

Troy nodded. "Fuckin' A. If I win this Open, hooray for me. You guys can just go home and play with yourselves."

The three of us laughed.

Harold stood up and said, "I have to go get my American Express card and buy a new putter. I *still* think that's my biggest problem right now."

The poets love to write about how women drive men bananas. Obviously those poets didn't play golf, the *real* torturer of men's minds and souls.

Some British sportswriter wrote an essay about golf, and one morning I read an especially eloquent paragraph of it to Nancy. She said, "Those limeys sure can write fancy, hey? I didn't understand a word of it, but it sure sounded good."

Hapless Harold Baumer always made me think of Pauly Wycliffe, a guy who used to play golf with us at Beaver Hills. He couldn't beat anyone, ever, and played with us for money. But he showed up often and we were always glad he came.

Pauly drove a truck for Yummy Goodies. Bayporters craved their snacks. I don't know how much money Pauly made at his job, but at Beaver Hills we shook him down.

If I drove past Beaver Hills and saw that Yummy

Goodies truck in the parking lot, I would pull in, get out my clubs and go say hi to Pauly.

I, or any other golfer, could give him every conceivable advantage and still hustle him until he had nothing but lint in his pockets. He would start out badly, get even worse and throw a temper tantrum so spectacular that I'd wish I had a Camcorder so I could put his flailing limbs on YouTube. Of course, the angrier he became, the worse he played.

Ry Semmens once bet Pauly a hundred dollars in a four-hole competition and gave Pauly a ridiculous advantage before they even started. Pauly would just have to get the ball into the cup *eventually* and he'd win their bet. Still, Pauly couldn't commit himself to accepting the challenge.

A cunning golfer and bettor, Ry always had some sort of angle not immediately apparent, and Pauly considered his offer too good to be true.

Ry had a reputation for being a savvy, imaginative character, sort of Beaver Hills' answer to Bobby Riggs. He could beat many of the boys even when he played on one leg, or with only one club, and his opponent got to choose which club he used. He had made remarkable drives with putters and sunk difficult putts with drivers. He had gotten out of sand traps or between trees while holding his club with one hand, using a pop bottle instead of a club, or keeping his eyes closed while making the shot.

He once showed up at Beaver Hills in a Fiberglas back brace. He said he'd just had surgery and thought a bit of golf would be therapeutic. He wore the back brace for months and had some Indian kid carry his things while he rode around Beaver Hills on a black motor scooter. Ry got many pats on the shoulder and good wishes, and plenty of bets that gave him substantial advantages. I backed off. I knew his back brace was a fake.

Ry saw everything, remembered most of it and bet on patterns he'd observed. He'd bet on the weather, the number of foreign cars on the road, or how many Chinks and Pakis were manning the counter at McDonald's as we went in for lunch.

Pauly knew about Ry and got suspicious at this golf challenge that seemed, on the surface, essentially a gift.

"So if I play a half-decent bunch of holes—"

"Then you win, fair and square," said Ry.

"How come you're giving me such a good deal?"

Ry shrugged. "We've beat you often enough. Time for you to win one and pocket some cash."

"So you want to give me this easy victory right here, right now?"

"Precisely," Ry said.

"I can't lose and you can't win. So why don't you just give me the money right now?" Pauly asked.

"I want to play some golf today. Doc says it's good for my health."

"I figure you're going to try suckering me into a side bet, like how many blades of grass we'll step on," Pauly said.

Ry shook his head. "No side bets. It's just what I've told you, nothing more."

Pauly frowned and thought for the longest time. Then he said, "No thanks. No way. My mum didn't raise any fool for a son."

What Pauly hated most of all on the golf course

was hitting the ball everywhere except where it needed to go.

His frame of mind would go from mild annoyance to blind rage.

Pauly, a strong man with a hard swing, would hit the ball into the trees the first time, then send it flying into the back yards of neighbors' houses. After picking up his ball, he'd scowl at it and speak to it as if scolding a misbehaving child.

"Are you enjoying this? Do you like making a bloody fool of me?" he would ask the inanimate object. "How would you like it if I just left you out here all alone?"

Sooner or later he would hit a ball so wildly that it strike, or barely miss, a car speeding past the golf course. Players then stopped betting on his performance.

Pauly would bring the head of his club to his face, and when he did so I couldn't help picturing Dirty Harry pulling a punk to his feet by his lapels so the two could have a nice little face-to-face chat.

"You are scum. You don't deserve to live."

We all knew then to run and hide.

Some of us would duck behind golf carts, while others would take cover behind trees, or just lie down and cover our heads.

Pauly's clubs would start flying in every direction. Foaming at the mouth like a rabid dog, and so insane with rage that his limbs jerked about like an epileptic's, Pauly would also curse like a 1970s B-movie black guy.

"Yo' momma, bitch!" he would scream. "Dumbass mofo fucked-up bullshit!"

Then he would calm down, tee the ball, assume his most proper stance and act like a serious golfer.

"Listen up," he would say to his club and ball. "Here's the deal. I'm gonna do my thing and hit this ball. If you fuck me over and this ball goes someplace bad…"

Pauly, whose only real problem at Beaver Hills was that he needed golf lessons, did his usual thing and hit the ball so awkwardly that I thought it might ricochet off a tree and hit him.

"No good goddamn freeloading son of a bitch retarded bigmouth know-it-all asshole jerk!"

He would shake the club and spit on it, then slam

it to the ground, as if it, and not he, were the problem.

By then, of course, the rest of us would be red-faced with laughter, holding our sides, doubled over like coronary victims.

Pauly might take a driver out to the parking lot and bash its head onto the concrete, swearing like a stevedore, his spittle shooting onto the pavement.

After a while, he'd clean up his mess, deposit his clubs, even the shattered and misshapen ones, into his golf bag. Getting his breath in between drags from an Export A, he would squint at us.

"So, are we going to golf, or just stand around here playing with ourselves?"

"I love your golf stories," Bronwen said to me. "Especially about those crazy characters at Beaver Hills."

I told her about golf because I knew of very little else. The game had become my work, livelihood and obsession. Golf and Teddy didn't separate, and she needed to know that if she hooked up with me, she had to be happy with Teddy Crossley, just an ordinary dude who didn't aspire to be more than, or different from, the humble Canadian golfer she beheld. If Bronwen wanted a tortured, brilliant philosopher, she needed to look elsewhere.

"Back at Oliver Johnson High School," I said to Bronwen, "I didn't read a textbook or pass a test. I didn't need to; as a star golfer, I got an automatic pass from my teachers because they didn't want to blow my ride."

"How accommodating of them," she retorted.

"Then I went to Northup University on a golf scholarship. The only decent grade I got, a C-plus in Canadian History, happened because the professor, a named Jarvis, played golf and I had helped him smooth out his swing a bit. I rarely attended any of my other classes, but I saw Jarvis regularly on golf-related matters, such as payment of golfing bets he'd lost to me, or to see if he had firmed up his plans to play eighteen holes with me on the weekend."

She shook her head in disgust.

Here is how I met Bronwen: I had slid my car into a pay parking lot in downtown Bayporte, discovered that I had no coins or cash, then hurried into a place called First Nations Art, to see if they could break a ten. Bronwen, the manager, said she could, and that's how we got started, over a tall cup of overbrewed coffee.

First Nations Art, as I recall, was a gallery featuring Native Canadian paintings: red, unsmiling faces and gorgeous sunsets and beaches. I wasn't sure how the place managed to pay its bills, since Bayporters weren't art connoisseurs and Bronwen had a decent-sized business in an expensive part of the city. At first I thought that the art gallery was just a front, that maybe they had half a ton of high-grade cocaine in the back to sell. Wouldn't have surprised me, if I knew Bayporte as well as I thought I did.

Brownen, sexy in a natural, folk-singer way, had a slimmed-down body with pert, perky breasts and a small bottom. She wore a black T-shirt and a pair of faded Levi's.

"Are you the boss around here?" I asked her. "I'm trying to find a poster of a kitten doing chin-ups with the caption, 'Hang in there, baby.'"

She invited me to sit and talk over a cup of java.

She kept me on her leash for nearly five years. We started getting it on very soon. I was her first jock; she, my first rich bitch. She turned me on to cannabis, sex toys and poppers. I offered to teach her golf; she said no.

At first, Bronwen impressed me as the most charming and solicitous of girlfriends. She gazed at me and said, "Thanks for being you."

She meant that by "being me" I had rescued her from the fate of marrying some Bayporte doofus who wanted nothing more from life than a cute wife, shiny toys and the admiration of everyone.

"Most people are indifferent and oblivious to reality," Bronwen said. "They don't want to see how things are because they're much happier being stuck in their own illusions."

"I can't understand you when you've stuck all those poppers inside my head," I replied. "Shit, I can't understand you at other times, either."

Don Morgan, Bronwen's father, a Northup almnus and prominent capitalist, seemed thrilled by his daughter's decision to marry me. "That's the most sensible thing she's ever done," he said. His wedding gift to us was a suite in a Bayporte highrise he had been unable to sell at its inflated price, along with a block of shares in a mining company that went bankrupt several months later.

Believing that our marriage, if it happened, would end in divorce, I tried to remind her of her myriad cultural interests that I did not share.

"The only thing I know about art," I said, "is that mostly it's done by tragic homosexuals who think everything in life has sexual connotations. They spend their whole lives saying, 'How come I'm queer? Why do I have to be this way?'

"Paintings are OK as long as they're about something. You need to look at it and say, 'Yeah, that's a nice house,' or whatever it is. It's no good if you look at it and say, 'I don't know what this painting is about. Someone needs to explain it to me.' There was this guy named Jackson Pollock, and he just splashed paint on a canvas and called it art. I could splash paint all over the place and call it art, but people would just tell me, 'Hey! Clean up your mess!'

"As for music, I like punk and heavy metal, but don't ask me to explain why. I guess it started when I was a kid, and I listened to whatever my friends had on the radio. I don't think it's good music. I don't know if there's such a thing as good music. It all sounds the same to me.

"Poetry? It's just a story told in rhymes. Don't have much use for that stuff, myself, although I kind of liked Poe's *The Raven*. That's a poem, isn't it?

"I've never been to the opera or ballet, and you couldn't drag me to one. I wouldn't know what was going on, so you'd have to explain it to me, and then I'd feel like a fool for needing an explanation. I'd have a better time at a local movie theater, watching people shoot each other.

"You," I said to Bronwen, "have already forgotten more than I've ever learned."

She pecked me on the nose. "Will you marry me?"

Since she seemed so eager to be with me, I introduced Bronwen to my life by taking her out on tour with me. We went to one of my favorite places: Pebble Beach in central California.

"You'll find art galleries, trendy shops and many

other amusements there," I told her. "I'll be perfectly OK if you decide to drive up to Big Sur instead of watching me play golf. Or you could go over to the Hog's Breath Inn and nurse a drink until Clint Eastwood showed up."

Bronwen sneered. "I have no interest in gawking at Clint Eastwood or any other movie star who has nothing better to do than hang out there."

We stayed at the Carmel Valley Inn, which I thought might make Bronwen feel at home because the place seemed to go out of its way to look unpretentious.

"This tournament doesn't really mean all that much," I said to her. "It's mostly a social thing to promote the sport and Pebble Beach. The pros usually end up with amateur partners who are too drunk to play decently, or even if they're sober, they can't play for shit.

"Unless you're Tiger Woods or Phil Mickelson, you must tee off first thing in the morning. It'll probably rain, or be so cold and windy that the wind will blow your airborne ball onto some course in Hawaii. It can also take you many hours to play eighteen holes because the guy in front of you is some famous performer who's too busy clowning around for the other golfers."

Alas, our trip to Pebble Beach happened before I deserved to play with someone like Gene Hackman. Early in my pro career, I would draw some guy from the South who got into this event because George C. Scott was sick.

The Southerner partnered with me would try to keep from sneering at me as he shook my hand. He'd come out there to play with John Daly or at least Troy Frisby.

I knew I had made an error in taking Bronwen there that first time because, as we drove along, we saw so many golfers swinging away or golfers driving along with golf bumper stickers on their cars.

Bronwen let out a derisive little chuckle.

"Wow," she said, "all these sad people out here, with nothing better do to than play with sticks and balls like little kids."

My first round of that tournament was something I will never forget. Unfortunately.

There I stood, on my first green at the legendary Pebble Beach, when I had a putt under ten feet. I tapped it just so, and for most of the way it looked pretty good, but the little fucker just wouldn't go in. Missed it by an inch.

Bronwen came up to me as I got ready to tee up for the next hole.

"What was *that* all about?" she asked, pointing in the direction of my failed putt.

"Almost but not quite," I said. "What a pisser, eh?"

"Shit," she said. "*I* could have made that putt, and I don't even *like* golf."

"Yeah, I kind of blew it, and I'm all busted up about it," I told her.

"Well," she said, "don't fuck up again like that."

I sighed, nodded and looked away.

"Oh," she added, "are you getting an attitude now?"

"Bronwen," I replied, "maybe you should go shopping, see what's going on in the area. I need to be out here by myself right now so I can focus."

She chuckled. "You need to focus on hitting a ball

into a cup?"

A little while later, I ended up in the rough. As I sorted through my clubs and deliberated about the best way of getting back onto the green, I heard Bronwen shout, "Why don't you just grab the ball and put it back on the grass like that other guy did a few minutes ago?"

I managed to hit the ball well onto the green, and Bronwen motioned for me to come over.

"Why didn't you just do as I said?" she asked. "You wasted all that time hitting the ball back onto the green when you could've just tossed it back out."

"Bronnie," I replied, "have you ever heard of something called *rules*? Throwing the ball instead of hitting it is considered *cheating*."

"I didn't know that," she said. "Some of these other players don't know that, either. You need to tell them these things." She backed off a bit after that, but if she saw me looking in her direction, she would smile and wave or blow me a kiss.

Things got much worse as the day wore on. My Southern partner and I played with Davis Love the Third and some guy named Tulio from Sacramento.

By then, I had gotten sloppy and tired. I must've been two or three over par, or even worse, but at the 16th or 17th I had a great chance at going under par until Bronwen yelled at me, "Ted! Check *that* out!"

"What?"

She pointed. "Can't you see it? A mountain lion!"

Yes, a half-grown mountain lion had bounded onto the golf course. Central California has its share of wildlife, and mountain lions are easy to find, if you go looking for them. The region also has its share of firearms enthusiasts, and I felt very little surprise when a few people in the crowd, or several, took out their handguns and fired a few rounds into the air, scaring the bejesus out of the big, beautiful cat, who sprinted off into the wilderness whence he had come.

I mopped the sweat off my forehead and putted the ball with very little care. I heard stifled groans as my ball missed the cup, and the tiniest smattering of applause as I finally tapped the ball in.

I went over to my wife, smoke curling out of my ears and my face as red as a beet.

"Fuck it all. It's all bullshit. Fuck every mountain lion and golf tournament in the whole motherfuckin' world."

I went on that way for a few minutes, swearing as profusely and imaginatively as I could. Bronwen looked shocked, then bemused. Finally she burst out laughing.

"Hello, Pauly Wycliffe," she said. "Glad to meet you. My husband has told me so much about you."

After taking a long, deep breath in a futile attempt at cooling off, I said, "Believe it or not, Bronnie, I'm not pissed off at you. Really. It's not your fault that a mountain lion got on the golf course. I'm mad at myself for not having the concentration and discipline to block out you and everything else, and just play good golf, like I'm supposed to.

"The truth is, this is the most difficult game in the world to play well, and I have to play my very, very best just to make enough money to live on. Can you understand that?"

"Then how come," she wanted to know, "Tiger Woods makes so much money and buys so much cool shit?"

At the Canadian Open in Placid Oaks, as I led the tournament, I kept thinking of Bronwen. I'm sure that the location had something to do with it. That place's quaint, charming loveliness often made Placid Oaks seem like Pebble Beach North, if Pebble Beach rained every other day.

Bronwen had been diagnosed with a very serious illness, and I wanted to know what would happen to her.

That evening, I decided not to party. I knew of several restaurants nearby that were good more often than bad. They had good Canadian beer, local steaks and fish and big, gooey desserts.

"I just don't want room service," Nancy said. "Some Paki brings it up and stares at my tits while you're signing the bill." She added, "I love going out with you while you're on TV every day because you're winning that golf thing. People recognize you. It's like you're *somebody*."

I sat in our Hotel Bayporte suite and watched reruns of *Family Guy* until Nancy went downstairs to the hotel's shopping arcade. She wanted to amuse herself by picking through the thousand-dollar crewneck sweaters at Elizabeth's boutique. Then I did what I had been wanting to do all day: I called Bronwen.

She answered her phone from her room in the Northup University Medical Center.

"Bronnie?" I said. "This is Teddy, your favorite golfing fool. I talked to Andrea, and she said you're in that place because they have state-of-the-art machines and doctors and they're your best chance of getting that big tumor shrunk down to nothing. Is that so?"

"My tumor," she said, "is about the size of a hockey puck. Too big to remove surgically, but they think the treatment they're giving me might shrink it down to where they can cut it out."

"How do you feel in general?" I asked.

"Not as bad as you probably think. I don't feel like someone who's about to croak."

"For real? Did they say you're about to croak?"

"Not yet. I'm feeling very optimistic about things in general. Maybe I'm just refusing to believe what the doctors say. Know what I did? I gave my tumor a name. I call it Troy."

"I'm sure he'll be flattered."

"I said to it, 'Troy, you don't scare me. You're just a cancer.'"

I grimaced. "That C-word really gives me the jimmies."

"It's just a word, Ted. Anyway, they tell me that Troy isn't getting any bigger and no part of it has broken off and made a new home for itself in another part of me."

"Well," I said, "that's something to be grateful for."

"Do you know why it hasn't spread? It's because I ordered it to stay put."

"The power of positive thinking."

"You know it," she said. "Most people, when the doctor gives them bad news, they start writing their wills and giving in to despair. But I say, 'Fuck *that* shit!'"

"You have the right attitude."

"I'm going to intimidate Troy into shrinking to the size of a dimple on a golf ball, then I'll call in the surgeon to take it out. Then I go on with life as if Troy had never invaded my beautiful body."

"You inspire me," I told her.

She chuckled. "You think this is bullshit? This is not bullshit, Teddy. I told Andrea that I'm young and strong, and I resent having cancer and I'm just going to kick the shit out of this tumor."

I laughed. "I hope you didn't tell Andrea that you named your tumor in honor of her husband."

"That's not all. After I kick Troy's ass and prove what *cretins* most doctors are, I'm going to take up golf and write trashy novels."

"You go, girl," I said. "Just don't ask me to read your novels. You know I'm not too good with big words."

"My first novel will be about a beautiful woman who beats cancer by fucking her brains out."

"She wins a Nobel Prize for discovering that sex cures cancer, depression and many other illnesses!" Then, "Bronnie, do you need anything I can provide?"

"Yeah, come see me after you win this one. Even *I* know that the Canadian Open in Bayporte is a big fucking deal. You're on TV all the time. Just don't choke and goof it up, OK?" She added, "No offense, but if Tiger Woods is playing, how come he isn't kicking your ass?"

I laughed. "I think Tiger is much less used to Placid Oaks than I am. He's having a bit of trouble adjusting to playing in Canada. I hope he keeps having trouble for a while longer."

"How's Troy doing?" she asked.

"You mean the golfer or the tumor?"

"One's as bad as the other." She snorted.

"The golfer is right up there with me and Tiger." Then, "I hear Nancy at the door. I'll call you tomorrow night. Stay strong and keep it real."

"And *you* make sure that *you* keep it together so that Tiger and Troy don't win."

Just then, Nancy entered our suite. I said into the telephone, "No, Tiger, I will *not* let you win the Open no matter how much money you pay me." Then I hung up as Bronwen heehawed into the receiver.

Bronwen disliked Troy Frisby from the moment they met. He dropped more names than a gossip columnist—all of the most famous golfers, plus Gretzky, Jordan, Montana, Jeter and half of

Hollywood. These A-list celebrities, he claimed, were his "peeps"; he was "tight" with them, and they "chilled" with him at Palm Springs and Pebble Beach.

"He's a wonderful guy," Bronwen said of Troy. "He'd sell you the shirt off his back."

In politics, and most other subjects, Bronwen and Troy had nothing in common.

She said, "Troy, it's hard for me to relate to someone whose world view is ME ME ME ME ME."

Bronwen knew I had no interest in politics. As I saw it, absolute power corrupted absolutely. Democrats and Republicans, conservatives and liberals—they were far more similar than they knew.

She enjoyed going to places with me and wearing buttons that said things like CONSERVE WATER—SHOWER WITH A FRIEND.

Listen: one time, we had a fun evening in New Orleans. The Frisbys and Crossleys received a dinner invitation from a couple of golf committeemen and their wives. They took us to some lively restaurant on Bourbon Street.

The moment I learned that one of our hosts went by the name Sonny, and found out that he worked in the oil business, sucking the crude out from under the Gulf of Mexico—he probably had something to do with the blow-out disaster that happened a few years later—I should have slipped under the table and crawled out of the restaurant. I don't think he would have noticed.

Every man I had ever met who still called himself Sonny would probably monopolize and dominate the conversation for the entire evening, with no intention whatsoever of shutting the fuck up.

So, over appetizers and cocktails, Sonny told us what he thought about many things. He laughed long and hard as he talked about going green (bad), gun control (even worse) and legalizing marijuana (good, as long as industry made lots of money off of it).

"Forget the lawyers," he said. "Let the *businessmen* run the country."

Bronwen looked at and listened to Sonny with an impassive expression. I winked and grinned at her, so she would know I appreciated her diplomacy. But she started frowning and swallowing as he started telling us about the time he checked into some ritzy hotel in Houston. He had to share an elevator, he said, with a bunch of "spooks" because the hotel had some kind of "jigaboo music" event happening that weekend.

"Filthy monkeys!" exclaimed Sonny's wife, pinching her nose. "They don't believe in taking a bath."

"We checked out," explained Sonny, "just as soon as we seen what was going on. I got hold of the manager and gave him what-for. He was thirty-five years old when I started in on him, and when I got done with him he looked about ready to retire."

Troy Frisby had a good laugh, and so did Sonny and his party.

Then Bronwen, in an even voice, said, "Showed them freakin' niggers that Uncle Charley is still boss, hey?"

Everyone fell quiet.

Bronwen then leaned over towards Sonny and said, "I want to ask you something. If I sat here and talked a bunch of odious nonsense and laughed at my own insipid jokes, would you resent my behavior?"

Sonny gave her his biggest, toothiest, most bulletproof smile. "No, sweetie, I wouldn't resent you. I would do my best to hear what you had to say.

But women aren't smart. They don't need to be. They just need to look good for their men. The men need to be smart. We run the world, you see."

Troy chuckled. "Amen to that."

"I totally disagree," Bronwen said, "with your opinions on the issue of blacks."

Troy chuckled again. "Sweetie, it's not an issue. It's a crisis. There are just too many niggers and spades. They outnumber the blacks."

Sonny nodded. "Amen to *that*, brother."

Sonny's wife said, "I think everyone deserves to have their dignity respected. But that doesn't mean I want any spooks sneaking up on me and robbing me at gunpoint when I'm out shopping."

Behind us stood our servers, two handsome young black men who must have overheard every word our party had spoken. Bronwen and I exchanged anxious glances. I sighed and wondered how many women shoppers in New Orleans worried about being robbed by "spooks."

Bronwen again leaned over towards Sonny and asked, "Do you know that our servers can hear what you're saying?"

Sonny shrugged. "Well, so what? They hear this kind of talk every day. Anyway, I tip pretty good, so I guess they'll overcome their hard feelings once they've got my money in their jeans."

Troy said, "Those people know their place. Do you know about Mike Tyson? He was the meanest, toughest badass and punk in New York City. So what do you do with him? You throw him in jail or make a boxer out of him. He hits hard, he's fearless and he doesn't notice if you punch back. So, for a while, he was the most exciting boxer alive. But then the perks of being 'Iron Mike' got him in trouble, because he was still a punk. That didn't change. If you want to know about blacks in pro sports and elsewhere, go to YouTube and watch some videos about William Shockley, the scientist."

"Oh," said Bronwen. "I guess Martin Luther King, Medgar Evers and Nelson Mandela were all just loudmouth punks."

"Yes," Sonny said. "That's *exactly* right. Especially King and Evers. They've contributed to America's current troubles."

Troy nodded. "Absolutely."

Bronwen rolled her eyes. "You're serious, too. That's what scares me. The world has millions of people who think as you do."

Sonny said, "We're just sitting here, having some supper and talking about the world as it is, not the way we want it to be."

"But," Bronwen said, "you're totally ignoring the whole issue of humanity and treating others with common courtesy."

Sonny frowned. "Well, I do believe in what Jesus said: 'Treat others as you would have them treat you.' Most of the time, I do just that, and I think others respect my decency. That's all I owe the rest of the world."

"I think," Bronwen told him, "that you need to have more empathy for African-Americans. You've treated them like second-class citizens—"

"*I've* treated them that way?" Sonny shot back. "I've treated them much better than they've treated *me*."

"Same here," said Troy.

"But if those spooks ever try to take what's mine," Sonny said, "or hassle my missus when she's out shoppin'…"

"You're so paranoid," Bronwen said. "Why?"

"No paranoia here," said Sonny. "Just two sensible men who know how it really is out there."

Sonny cleared his throat. "Now, sweetness, if you insist on hearin' me defend myself, let me say a few more things. I'll lose a little sleep now and then because the liberals in Washington are gonna start tellin' me I have to hire a certain number of spooks when those spooks don't know how to do the job, or Uncle Sam will fine me or put me out of business. I'm losin' sleep over a few other things, such as how a few dummies who load up on guns and go out on shooting sprees will end up makin' guns harder to get for those law-abidin' citizens who own and use guns the right way."

Sonny nodded and said nothing more, looking as smug as a debating champion who had just left his opponent sweating and speechless.

Bronwen smirked and said, "Fucking unreal."

The Southern wives stared at her.

Sonny gave her a prim little smile. "Now, I like my dinner guests to act like ladies and gentlemen."

"I hear ya, big guy," replied Bronwen. "You back off with the racial slurs and I'll stop dropping F-bombs. Truce?"

The Southern wives rolled their eyes.

"In fact," Bronwen continued, draining her White Russian, "I'll just get up and mosey along and let you folks finish your conversation down here in good ol' Dixie."

"Nice attitude," said Troy.

Bronwen glowered. "What's that, goof?"

Troy turned to Sonny. "We're from Canada, where the word 'goof' is a particularly offensive insult. If I wasn't such a gentleman and she wasn't a woman, I would punch her out for calling me such a name."

Bronwen guffawed. "'If I wasn't such a gentleman, I'd punch her out.' What a wussy."

Then she got up and left. I hurried after her, but she eluded me. Outside, two out of three cars seemed to be taxis, so I assumed she had gotten into one.

"I suppose," I said when I returned to our table, "that she went back to our hotel, so I better go there too."

"Canadian women," Troy said, "can be very

difficult."

Sonny shrugged. "Most of the Canadian women I've met have been nice enough. Maybe she's just havin' one of them female things."

"Bronwen," said Andrea, "has lots of intelligent opinions. She's one of the smartest people I know."

Troy said, "Just finish your dessert."

Sonny's wife said, "I think the media are to blame for so many problems. They take things like the Rodney King beating or the Canadian cops who Tasered that man to death at the airport, and the media just show it again and again. They get everyone all worked up and angry."

"Ted," Sonny said, "I apologize if I offended your lady with my talk. It's just conversation. It doesn't mean anything."

Sonny's wife said, "That young woman has quite a set of opinions, and when you disagree with her, it's like you're spitting in her face. It's not your fault."

I nodded. "Bronwen is a very strong-willed person, but she means well. She wants to save the world and make everything beautiful. I hope she didn't spoil everyone's evening."

"Not at all," said Sonny's wife. "My supper was delicious."

I went back to our hotel and found Bronwen in front of the TV, eating a big frothy dessert she'd bought at the ice cream parlor downstairs.

"Hi," I said. "I can tell that life with you will rarely be boring."

She swallowed a spoonful of froth and said, "Did I do wrong? Are you ashamed of me?"

I put my hands on my hips and took a deep breath. "You could have handled things…differently. You could have just gotten lost in your own pleasant thoughts. You could have changed the conversation to who Tom Cruise is going to marry next or how many more babies Madonna will adopt. I know Sonny is a racist prick, and he's a bad golfer, too, but he's also a rich guy and a generous supporter of the PGA. You could have gotten mad at him over dinner and then vented on me later. By getting mad at them, you just made them feel very superior to you."

"Ted," she said, "I want to lay a bit of philosophy

on you."

"I hope this isn't going to be one of those Socrates or Nietzsche or Kant things that you have to explain to me. They give me a headache and I still don't understand them."

She smiled. "Nothing like that. It's just this bit of wisdom that I occasionally forget."

"Let's hear it."

"There are two basic rules to life. The first is, don't sweat the small stuff—"

"And the second rule is, it's all small stuff."

Bronwen nodded. "Think you can remember that? And if you see *me* forgetting it, be sure to remind me."

PART 3:

SO LONG, SUCKA

HOLE IN ONE

5

Saturday at Placid Oaks became a special day for me. A few things made it different for me than for millions of other people everywhere.

Bronwen's illness totally freaked me out. It just refused to leave her lung and my mind. Look, if a nasty-ass cancer could move into the body of a vibrant, exuberant, brainy young woman, why were the rest of us still alive and in decent shape?

In spite of myself, I played some damn fine golf and finished just under 70. Alas, so did Troy Frisby, so he remained a close second to me at the Canadian Open in Bayporte.

Due to the unrelenting international publicity of being first and second, Troy and I nearly punched it out in the locker room. Golfers, unlike hockey players and pugilists, don't hit each other. We use profanity and throw our caps and clubs, but we never resort to fisticuffs. A guy could get hurt that way.

On Saturday, I learned something about Nancy that would shake me up, regardless of the outcome of the golf tournament, or Bronwen's illness, or anything else. Nancy would show me her true colors.

Troy had started annoying me when we went into the press tent to answer the sports reporters' bullshit questions on Saturday afternoon.

"I know that God will determine who wins this tournament," he said, looking as peaceful as a Hindu cow. "I have prepared myself for this competition to the very best of my ability, but ultimately He will decide who wins, and I accept that."

He went on like that for a while, and he mentioned that he'd had several conversations with God about this tournament.

I asked, "Did He say anything about *me*?"

Everyone chuckled except Troy.

"Troy," asked one of the reporters, "what is your religion?"

"It's whatever you want it to be," I blurted.

"I am a Lutheran," Troy said.

Once we got into the locker room, I started in on him about his nonsense in the press tent.

"I don't know if I can win this thing," I told him, "now that I know you have an invisible helper, and He's pretty tough to beat."

"I gave them some good soundbites," he said.

"Doesn't your conscience nag at you?" I asked him.

"For what?"

"For that crap you said to the reporters just now."

Troy scratched his head. "What crap? I just told them how I felt. I was honest and sincere. Don't you believe in God, Teddy?"

"Troy," I said, "you told the world out there that you're a Lutheran, but you wouldn't know the first thing about it even if Martin Luther himself came back from the dead and explained it all to you."

"When I was growing up," Troy said, "my mum and dad raised me as a Lutheran."

"Did they ever take you to church?"

"Oh, I'm sure they did."

"Did you *listen* to the sermons?" I asked him.

"I guess I did. Anyway, what's that got to do with playing golf right now?"

"Everything, according to the book of Troy," I

told him. "Didn't you listen to yourself in the press tent? All that God talk? You said He was gonna help you win this thing."

"Well, maybe He will." He paused. "I did not say I would win. I did not say that. I just said I would do my best, like everyone else, and that if I was meant to win, I would win."

"You *definitely* gave those reporters the impression that you believed you and He were tight and that your special relationship with Him might just influence the outcome of this Open because you were His fair-haired boy."

Troy pointed at me. "Are you questioning my sincerity?"

"I'm saying that you better play some *heavenly* golf tomorrow or *I'm* gonna win this thing."

Troy snarled at me. "Someone should kick your ass."

"When you can find the man for the job, send him over."

He kept snarling as he slammed his locker's door and threw some clothes onto the floor. "See you out there, douche bag."

"That's not a very Christian attitude," I retorted.

That night, I got gooned in the hotel's lobby bar and decided to call Bronwen again.

"Bronnie? Sorry it's so late and I'm so drunk, but the barman made me drink half a bottle of Canadian Comfort. It's been a weird day."

"I saw you on TV," she said. "I watched most of the tournament. Your taste in clothes has improved."

"Glad you approve. When I took over the lead a few days ago, I was glad I saved my spiffiest threads for the weekend, when everyone would be watching me. I'll have to sort through my wardrobe to see what else I have left to wear."

"Just don't go out there looking like Troy Frisby," she admonished me. "He dresses like a bloody pimp."

"He acts like one, too," I said.

She laughed.

"Bronnie, I want to tell you something. I'm going to play my best tomorrow. Better than my best, in fact. There should be a law against playing this well. Do you know what I've shot this week? Low seventies and high sixties. At Placid Oaks! Nobody can play that well on that course. I'm at two-oh-nine overall, and Tiger Woods is at two-fifteen, and he can't believe he's six shots back of me. Neither can everyone else."

Bronwen laughed. "I guess right now it's pretty amazing to be Teddy Crossley."

"A little scary, too. All this attention that I'm not used to? Everyone wants me to pose with them for a cell phone picture. People are sticking microphones in my face and asking me everything except how often I jerk off. I'm being interviewed by *The New York Times* and I'm having cocktails with the American and Canadian media bosses."

"Are the other golfers," Bronwen asked, "being supportive of you?"

"Not exactly. Tiger Woods thinks my clubs are illegal, and that's why I'm hitting the ball so hard and straight. Tiger forgets that I'm from Bayporte and have played at Placid Oaks many times, so I know the course a bit better than he does. Troy is on the rag because he thinks there's a definite possibility that he's going to finish number two, and to him that really sucks. McIlroy and Mickelson are scratching their heads because they've never even heard of me."

"How's Nancy enjoying all this attention? Are they taking pictures of her big boobs and heart-shaped bum?"

I ignored this. "I'm getting creeped out by looking up at the leader board and seeing my own name at the top. We're not fucking around here, you know what I mean? This is the big time, the Canadian Open, Placid Oaks, late in the game, and I'm *winning* the damn thing. The officials are staring at me all the time because the big guys—Nicklaus, Palmer, Trevino, Hogan, Woods—usually win these things, and who the fuck am *I* to be on top?

"I know that I need to keep my mind on each shot, because if I screw up even a little bit, Troy Frisby and Tiger Woods and the other guys will eat me alive. Winning the Canadian Open would be a dream come true for me, and I don't know if I'll ever come this close again.

"Did I tell you that Harold Baumer has been here, cheering me on? He didn't make the cut, but he's stuck around to give me moral support. I would look over and see him standing with the other spectators behind the ropes. When we made eye contact, he would pump his fist, to remind me to stay hungry and not to lose my edge.

"When I would tee up a ball and haul off and hit it just right, he would yell, 'Hole in one, baby! Hole in one!'

"When the hole in one didn't happen and I was somewhere on the green, trying to get closer to the cup, I'd hit it and he would yell, 'Get in there! Get in there!'

"Late in the day, as I traipsed along and stood at the tee, wiping the sweat off my face, Harold was close enough to say, 'Easy.' Just that one word, but I nodded. I needed to pace myself."

I paused and added. "He's more pumped up about this event than Troy and I are. But would you *listen* to me? I'm just going on about golf and myself while you're the one with real-life troubles."

"It's all right, Ted. You're doing me a favor by talking about your success in the Open. It gets my mind off of myself for a few minutes." She added, "I'm getting nervous about the Open, too, Ted. I want you to win *so* badly because you're so close to doing it. Something big and special is happening over there at Placid Oaks, and you're in the middle of it. Those are the moments that make life so thrilling. Am I making sense?"

"Yes," I half-lied.

"Tomorrow, either you'll win the Canadian Open or someone else will—and frankly, I would much rather see Fred Couples do it than Troy—but whatever happens, it will be one of the greatest experiences of your life. I envy you because you've spent your entire life doing something you love, and most of us aren't that lucky."

"You sound so upbeat and optimistic," I told her. "Are you feeling good about your own challenges?"

"Damn right," she said. "I may lose this challenge, and some people have been heartless enough to say I'll be dead soon, but I'm fighting like hell and have never felt so alive. Weird, eh?"

"Well, *your* adversary is much tougher than Troy Frisby or even Tiger Woods." Then, "Bronnie, I'm starting to believe in that 'power of positive thinking' stuff. I've had personal, firsthand experience with it. I've putted the ball and more or less *willed* the little bastard to drop in."

Bronwen laughed. "Then if it's all in the head, why don't you hit a hole in one every time out?"

"Because," I said, "it's *partly* in the mind, and partly in the club, and partly in the muscles."

"Just wondering," she said. "What would you do if you were at Beaver Hills, betting against Ry Semmens, and you tried to will your putt into the cup but it wouldn't go?"

"I would throw a temper tantrum and go looking for Pauly Wycliffe."

She laughed for a long while.

"Shit, Bronnie," I continued. "You're over there in that hospital room and I'm over here, and I feel like I've let you down…"

"No. We got together. Our life was good as often as bad. It didn't work out, but we had some fun. It's terrific that we can talk on the phone and still be here for each other."

"I wonder," I said, "why He wants you back so soon. You've been neither great nor awful. You've been like the rest of us."

"I wonder," she replied, "why *you're* probably going to win the Canadian Open even though Tiger

Woods, Rory McIlroy and Troy Frisby are all trying to beat your ass. You know why you're in the lead? Because it's your time right now. Know why I'm on my way out? Because maybe it's *my* time. Nothing fair or logical about any of it. Do you remember those philosophy books I could never get you to read? They mostly dealt with the utter unfairness of life."

We both fell silent.

"I've been thinking," I told her, "about Steve Jobs. He had six billion dollars, and in his fifties he died of cancer. All that money and the doctors couldn't save him. Fuck." I sighed. "I shouldn't talk about this shit after I've been drinking. It depresses me."

"Too bad for Steve Jobs," Bronwen said.

"I hate the rich and powerful," I told her. "They have us by the balls. They make us do things we hate to do. They make us do things that make us hate ourselves. Go to work at an awful job or starve to death in the street. Go fight a war and die for your country, or come back shell-shocked. If you refuse to go fight, go to jail—go directly to jail."

"We live in a diseased society, Ted," Bronwen said. "I'm afraid it's been that way for a very long time."

I harrumphed. "I get fed up with it. People who drink booze and smoke cigarettes are *passionately* against the legalization of marijuana. Uncle Sam invades Iraq in retaliation for the World Trade Center. The troops come home mentally or physically damaged and have a hard time getting professional help or financial aid."

Bronwen said, "Everything's fucked. Have you tried to buy a car lately? Tens of thousands of dollars for a piece of junk. They're made of aluminum and they break down within months so you'll keep your mechanic busy."

"Absolutely," I said. "That applies to a hundred other consumer products. But if you're a rich asshole, you don't mind because you can afford to buy a hundred more of everything. You travel all over the world and stay at the ritziest hotels but you never tip the bellman."

"Too right. What's a person to do about it?"

"Either you're a member of the lucky sperm club and you're born into a world of luxury or privilege, or you're like Bill Gates or Steve Jobs, and you get involved in a very lucrative industry *very early on*." Then, "Shit, Bronnie, this cancer thing that's happening to you? It's so outrageous. It makes my blood boil.

"By the way," I asked her, "are you getting sick of listening to me bitch like this?"

"Doesn't bother me," she said. "I don't have anything better to do. But maybe *you* should get into bed and sleep. Big day tomorrow."

"I'm not worried about sleep. I play better with a hangover. I swing the club less aggressively." I sighed. "But who cares? It's just a fuckin' game."

I ragged some more about the rich pricks I had known, who treated the rest of humanity like maggots and got away with it. Those pricks did little work and had endless contempt for those who put in forty-hour weeks. The pricks paid no taxes and waltzed through life in glowing health. Finally, I told her, "Those pricks send their progeny to private schools where the brats learned that the masses *deserved* to work hard, stay poor and die young."

Fearing that I would imminently burst into tears, I said goodnight and hung up the phone. During the last part of our conversation, I nearly told Bronwen about Nancy and Troy.

After my confrontation with Troy, during which he'd half-threatened to punch me out but then lost his nerve, I returned to the clubhouse and met up with some of the network honchos, and they invited me for cocktails. An hour later, they went on with their business and I went to check my emails.

While I'm no cyberwizard, I know how to use my iPhone and Mac Pro, and as a public figure, I see enough cell phones and Camcorders pointed at me when I'm golfing. I know enough not to grab my junk, scratch my ass or do anything else I don't want the world to see on YouTube.

So, when I opened my emails and discovered that someone had sent me a video file, I grew apprehensive. It's easy enough for private people to get the email addresses of public people—mostly because we public people really put our contact information out there, along with blogs in which we tell our adoring public everything except how often we take a dump.

A video file is the kind of thing you get in your

email whenever someone wants to blackmail you. A video file says, *Here is something I think you should see.*

I opened it and found footage of Placid Oaks. The camera zoomed in towards the edge of the trees and shrubs that I recognized as around the sixth hole.

I also recognized the man leaning against one of the oak trees, well concealed from anyone who might have been following the golf match. His name was Troy Frisby, and I chuckled at the sight of his colorful clothes that are half off. Troy was banging away at some cutie with her back to me.

Troy had put in a full day of golf, but there he stood, back on the course, or close to it, doing the wild thing with that little lass.

The footage showed them in a very deep kiss, as if they were trying to suck out each other's tongue.

Troy squeezed one of the girl's plump, firm breasts. He used his other hand to grope her heart-shaped bottom.

I couldn't get an especially clear look at her face, even when she turned her head or I tilted my computer. Therefore, I couldn't go into a courtroom and swear that I absolutely, positively knew the name of the woman I watched Troy boff.

But I knew, I completely fucking *knew*, that the girl being pronged by my best friend was my wife, Nancy Lynn fucking Crossley.

Of course, I didn't tell anyone about it, just as Nancy stayed mum. I didn't even know if the person who'd emailed me the footage knew Troy was diddling my missus.

But I kept watching, not feeling particularly embarrassed or humiliated, but turned on and voyeuristic, as if I'd orchestrated this freak scene between my pal and my gal. Now I sat alone, beating off to it.

So I checked them out, thinking about Troy the cocksman, who had screwed one woman over the Pacific Ocean while his drunk wife snoozed a dozen feet away. He had done it, with a woman whose name he had never learned, in a loan car during a summertime traffic jam in downtown Toronto. He'd once gotten a blow job—or a hand job, or maybe both—from his dental assistant while his dentist worked on a patient in another room.

So now he stood just out of sight in Placid Oaks

during the Canadian goddamn Open, shagging Teddy's old lady? What the fuck was up with *that*?

I watched on as my buddy unzipped my woman's shorts and she shimmied out of them, her shapely bare cheeks jiggling in the Bayporte humidity.

I could see her hands at the fly of his apple-green pleated slacks and pull out his member. I thought of a bumper sticker that read GOLFERS SWING STIFF SHAFTS. Troy certainly did.

There stood my Nancy, with her shorts and undies on the ground, private parts being caressed by the breeze at Placid Oaks with Troy Frisby's stiff shaft in her soft, uncallused hand.

The sunlight appeared to struggle through the stubborn Bayporte cloud cover. *Money shot*, I thought, and giggled despite myself.

I swallowed hard and forced myself to keep watching. Incredible, I told myself, that they were at a golf course—Placid Oaks!—during a golf tournament—the Canadian fucking Open!—and they were going to Do It—standing up!

In the bedroom with Bronnie, during our marriage, I had said, "I can't screw standing up. I'd get a hernia."

Troy had no such problem. He leaned against a tree trunk, hoisted up Nancy by her bum, and they started pumpin' away like nobody's bloody business. Throughout the action, Troy had his tongue down her throat and his eyes wide open, like a porno stud watching the director's hand gestures.

Afterwards, Troy tucked in his junk and Nancy crawled back into her things. They just stood there, sharing a Player's Light and chatting a bit, maybe laughing about how they had just cuckolded poor old Teddy.

Troy looked at his Rolex and said something. They did another of their big kisses, she squeezed his shaft, he patted her bum, and the two parted.

A little voice inside my head said, "We'll be back with more action at Placid Oaks after these public service announcements from the Ad Council about the dangers of unprotected intercourse with someone else's wife."

By the end of Saturday, when I couldn't find

Nancy at Placid Oaks, I knew she had taken a taxi back to our hotel. She couldn't be bothered to wait around for me while I golfed. As I headed to the parking lot to get my car, I kept fantasizing about Nancy and Troy: her long blonde hair cascading down her back as she orally polished Troy's big stiff club.

As much as my wife's behavior enraged me, I would keep my hands to myself. I refused to hit a woman. I kicked things and sometimes hurt my feet. I swore like a truck driver. Like most other male golfers, I wimped out at the prospect of hitting other men, especially when they looked angry enough to punch me out. Fortunately, I had some time to be alone and think as I drove back to the hotel.

I pondered the myriad times, in a handful of cities, that Nancy said she would rather go shopping or spend the day on a tour bus than cheer me on at the golf tournament. On those occasions, had she really gone sightseeing or shopping, or had she been up to something else?

Naturally, when we first met, I knew she had gotten around a bit and had her share of boyfriends and maybe a few girlfriends, too. But I'd assumed she was better than those chippies who had routinely thrown themselves at every man who'd had a bit of success and made a few bucks.

In the car, I started grinning at the ludicrousness of my predicament. Why get ulcers or hypertension over this matter? Just let it be another one of life's not-so-subtle ironies.

Hey, Nancy? How's my cheatin' wife today? Did you stoop for the troops? Did you bang for the gang? Did you offer yourself to the other golfers at Placid Oaks? Was Troy the only taker? Has Tiger Woods met you yet?

I mocked my marriage because it was a mockery.

Back at the hotel, I discovered her in Elizabeth's boutique, trying to talk herself into buying herself a few nice things with my American Express card.

"Hello, stranger," she said, turning around and smiling. "I watched the golf in the clubhouse with Andrea, then had a couple in the bar with some of the other golf widows. So, where've you been, hey?"

"I've been here and there," I said. "I spent a while checking my emails."

"You're sure playing good golf this time. Everyone thinks you're going to win this one." She added, "I can't wait to see what happens tomorrow. If it's not you, it will be Troy. Isn't that terrific? At least Tiger won't do it. He'll have to wait for the next one."

"I'm thirsty," I said. "Let's go get a drink."

We entered the bar just off the shopping arcade. Downtown Bayporte had more bars than it needed. Visitors must have thought Canadians were a bunch of lushes. Maybe we were.

"They showed quite a lot of you and Troy on TV." Nancy chuckled. "Troy really sticks out there in his crazy clothes, eh?"

I nodded. "He sure is a colorful character."

We got a table for two in a dark section of the bar. I needed as much privacy as possible, and felt relieved that we had no third chair for another golfer to plop into once he'd recognized me and invited himself to sit with us. He'd crack jokes, touch my arm every ten seconds and ask me why I used Pings instead of Nikes.

I sat and listened as Nancy talked throughout our first round of drinks.

"I'm going to spend tomorrow at Placid Oaks with Andrea. I'll cheer you on while she cheers him on. It'll be OK. We know each other well enough that the losing wife will support the winning one."

"Do you know where they're having dinner?" I asked.

She nodded. "With his agent and manager. They're going to talk about endorsements and tax shelters."

I grinned. "Sounds like Troy doesn't know he's going lose this Open."

She rolled her eyes. "He's *such* an optimist. He has deals up the wazoo. He promotes one brand of cigarettes even though he smokes another. It doesn't matter to him. He's the spokesman for some resort in Arizona he's never stayed nor played at."

I ordered another round of drinks.

Nancy pouted. "Teddy, you don't seem thrilled about the Open. Are you coming down with something?"

I nodded. "I've got a very bad case of heartbreak. I found a little while ago that the woman I live with and love with, the woman who is my wife, has been loving somebody else."

She frowned. "Excuse me?"

"My wife and my best friend have been screwing."

She pointed at my glass of Canadian Comfort over ice. "Are you pissed? How many of those have you had?"

I drained my glasses and signaled for another one. "I'm just wondering: Does Troy do it better than I do it? His dick is bigger than mine. Does size *really* make that much of a difference?"

Nancy looked down at the table. "Hmm. Interesting. So…you think I've been cheating on you with Troy."

"No, I don't *think* so, I *know* so. I know about you and him by the trees at Placid Oaks, and I'm wondering if there have been other men. I'm also wondering if you think Troy considers you anything more than just another notch on his stiff shaft."

"Asshole," she muttered. I didn't know if she meant him or me. "I don't know who told you what, but the fact that you *believe* it doesn't say much for you or me."

"And the fact that you've been messing around with somebody else means that we have a serious problem."

She squared her shoulders and said, "I don't know where you're getting your information from, but I *do* know this: I may be Wife Number Three, but I know about Helga and Bronwen, and I can say that in all ways I've been Wife Number One. I don't throw tantrums. I keep my tummy tight and my titties up. Whenever you're on the rag because you've blown a lead on the golf course, I try to be nice to you. You don't know what a good wife you have."

I smirked and said, "Oh, so it's all *my* fault. *I* drove you to seek solace in another man's weenie."

She lit a Player's Light and blew out a huge stream of smoke. "Who told you these lies about me, anyway?"

I started to tell her about the video file on my computer, when some smiling cretin came up to us, grabbed my hand and gave it a pump, then introduced himself as Toronto Tony, sales manager of Metro Toronto BMW or Mercedes, or maybe Volvo.

"I'm the biggest golf fan you'll ever meet," he said. "I'm no Teddy Crossley, but I've played all over North America. I never get sick of Placid Oaks. It's as fine a course as you'll find. Let me sit down and buy you two a drink for good luck. I know just about all the guys on the tour, and would be proud to have them all as my personal friends." He clamped his hand down on my shoulder and said to Nancy, "This is a good man. He's getting pretty bloody famous, but I'm sure he'll never get so full of himself that he'll refuse to have a drink with the rest of us. I *love* it when a Canadian is winning for a change—"

Nancy blew out a stream of smoke and said, quietly and sweetly, "Tony? If you don't go away right now, I'm going to kick your balls up through the roof of your mouth."

Toronto Tony stopped smiling and looked at me as if to say, *Are you going to let her speak to me that way?* Then he skulked away.

I laughed and said to Nancy, "Well, you do have your moments. Too bad they're so few and far between." Then, "Not to sound like a TV cop, but do you know where you were on Friday afternoon?"

Her eyes narrowed. "Why do you ask?"

"Just answer the question."

"I think," she said, "that I left Placid Oaks early. I

went out to Northup University and took a nice long walk. I hadn't visited that place in ages."

"Do you remember what you were wearing?"

"Something very chic and revealing. You seem to like me dressed that way."

"Troy, too," I said.

"I get a lot of attention when I dress in a sexy way," she told me. "Like I said, I dress to make you happy and turn you on."

I sipped at my Canadian Comfort over ice and described the itty-bitty movie I had seen of my wife's infidelity. I told her that my favorite porn queens— Ginger Lynn, Megan Leigh and Jenna Jameson— could not have played a better scene.

"You're trying to make a fool of me, Nancy. I know my wife's face and hair and body when I see her in someone's home video that they send to me."

She frowned and pouted as she stared into her drink, then she regarded me with much seriousness as she squared her shoulders again.

"Do you," she asked with fake outrage, "think that tramp in the video was *me*?"

I drained my drink, had our server bill our

cocktails to our room, and told Nancy I was going up to our suite to have a nice long sleep. The rest of my evening would consist of a bath, dinner and enough Canadian Comforts over ice to render me unconscious.

"We can talk about the big picture later," I said. "But one thing is for sure: After this Open is a done deal, things between us are going to change."

Up in our suite, Nancy made faces and refused to speak to me, as if I'd spat in her eye and called her a whore. When our room service dinner arrived, she muttered to herself as she devoured her food. As soon as she finished her chocolate cheesecake, she locked herself in the bedroom.

I smiled at the sight of the locked bedroom. I could get nice and drunk, call Bronwen and sort through old memories.

I concluded that I had gone through three bad marriages. Obviously, I didn't do marriage well. Did I do golf well? No. I didn't do life that great, either. Many people younger than myself did most things much better than I, and I've always had a competitive spirit. Long ago, I convinced myself that I had more brains than most other people I had met. I had yet to read an entire book, but so what? I could outplay everyone at Beaver Hills, shake down any guy in any poker game and smell another guy's bullshit as if bombast and exaggeration had odors. Alas, for a smart guy, I'd certainly let enough women make a chump of me.

Nancy's little attitude reminded me of Wife Number One.

If Helga had ever wanted to lay a friend of mine—Troy, for example—she would have said something like, "Teddy, let's call Troy and Andrea. We can smoke a little reefer, drink a little wine and see what comes up."

I recalled a night many years back when my friends and I sat at a booth in Paul's Submarine Stop. We drank beer and talked about, as Julie Andrews sang in *The Sound of Music,* a few of our favorite things.

We had this conversation at Paul's because we

were bored shitless and had exhausted all of our more meaningful topics, such as how well the Northup Kodiaks would cope with their injured quarterback or when Paul would increase the price of his steak sandwich.

One of us said she wanted to travel all over the world and rarely, if ever, return to Bayporte. She'd already seen and done everything good in the city. Another of us said he couldn't imagine living anywhere but here; he couldn't live without his daily fix at Paul's.

"*My* turn-on," I told them "is whacking a little dimpled ball across a vast expanse of grass."

Helga spoke up. "There's nothing half as sweet on God's green earth as getting it on with a sexy lover."

About half a dozen of us sat at that table. Everyone looked at each other, but not at her. A few faces turned red or white.

"What?" Helga asked, looking around. "Did I say the wrong thing?"

Willy Wark turned to her. "Sis, how would you like to make it with a Paki?"

She shrugged. "I did, once. Wasn't much. I've had

lots better."

"I didn't know that," I muttered.

"You guys know Baldy Ghurana from Oliver Johnson High?" she asked. "Well, he chatted me up when I was feeling really horny. I don't know if he counts as a true Paki, because he was born in Canada."

Willy said, "You better be lyin', 'cause if you're tellin' the truth, there's gonna be one dead Paki on the streets of Bayporte tomorrow."

Helga snarled at her brother. "Well, you asked and I answered. Anyway, you've stuck your thing into lots of non-white holes, too."

He snarled back. "Yeah, but that's different. I'm Willy, you're Helga."

"Don't be mad at Baldy," said Helga. "I'm a temptress. I seduced him. He had some pot, and we got into his car so he could show me how to smoke it. We got stoned, he got friendly and I said OK."

Willy said, "Instead of killin' him, maybe I'll just castrate him. Bein' unable to fuck? Shit, that would be worse than dyin'."

I then saved Baldev "Baldy" Ghurana's life, or at

least his testicles. I liked Baldy; we both golfed at Beaver Hills. "Willy, Helga's just teasing you. Baldy's never gone near her. Isn't that so, Helga?"

Helga leaned over and ran a hand over her brother's bristly haircut. "Just teasin', William. I know Baldy from school, but we've never fucked or nothin'."

"You shouldn't say those things," Willy said. "I was about to go tear off his ball bag, and he wouldn't have even known why. A guy likes to keep his ball bag if he can."

We sat there and drank Diefenbaker beer and talked about things like why the movie theaters didn't have better shows, why movie tickets cost so much and why the "golden topping" they put on the popcorn tasted like piss.

"Want to know who I *did* fuck?" Helga asked. "I did it with Joe Garcia, the bartender at the Western Inn. He's Mexican or something."

"Did he show you a good time?" Willy asked.

She shrugged. "He liked it more than I did. I said 'Yes' and then 'No,' but he just kept going."

Willy drained his bottle of Diefenbaker. Then he

slammed the bottle against the edge of the table. It shattered into a nasty weapon of jagged brown glass. Many people looked in our direction, including Paul, the owner, but nobody said anything, for the simple reason that you didn't antagonize Willy Wark.

Willy let out a huge belch and said, "Garcia raped my sister. He must die." He added, "There's enough time for another beer or two, but then I have to get over to the Western Inn and have a chat with him about the proper way to treat a lady."

"He has a switchblade, Willy," Helga said. "He's in a gang."

"Nice for him."

I really didn't give a damn about Willy and his plans to kill Joe Garcia. I knew Garcia as a short, stocky punk with a big mouth. Helga said he had a gang affiliation; I didn't believe that any gang worth joining would have him as a member.

We all went with Willy to the Western Inn's bar.

As we stood behind him, Willy said to Joe Garcia, "How's it goin', goof?"

Joe smiled at him. "Good. What can I get you and your friends to drink?"

Willy leaned on the bar and said, "No, I'm not thirsty. I'm just looking for some fucking goof asshole Mexican who likes to rape white girls, because my sister Helga here got raped by some brown fucking asshole goof who looked a lot like you."

Joe Garcia didn't move or do anything else. He just stood there and kept smiling. I admired him for that. Most guys would have passed out or pissed their pants after hearing all that trash talk from Willy Wark.

"I think," continued Willy, "that I'm going to fuck you up tonight. Are you man enough to come outside with me and fight like a man, or are you going to be a brown Mexican faggot wimp and fight me with that switchblade you always carry?"

Joe still wore his big professional smile as he said, "No, guy, I got rid of that switchblade. I found a new weapon. Wanna see it?"

He reached down and came up with a .45 automatic and thrust it into Willy's chest.

"Listen, guy," Joe said, "if I pull this trigger, it's gonna blow your heart, lungs and ribs all over this bar and it'll take a week to clean it all up. So why don't you take your friends and your tramp of a sister and go away, and we'll both forget that this ever happened."

Amazingly, Willy stood up straight, turned around and walked out. We followed him.

Out in the parking lot, everyone stayed quiet. I hoped Willy wouldn't blow off some steam by punching me out. I thought of suggesting that he hotwire Garcia's car, drive it over to a chop shop and make a few bucks at Joe's expense.

But Willy just stood there and stared at the ground. Finally, he shrugged and almost grinned.

"That," he said, "was the first time I've ever backed down from a fight."

Throughout the years, I have never told anyone just how deeply I valued Helga. I didn't tell Bronwen, even when she interrogated me like a psychologist. I suppose I kept things to myself because I grew up as a James Dean wannabe—brooding, detached, convinced that expressing weakness or emotional pain was uncool. I did not often take Helga into my arms and tell her that I loved her. Maybe she needed that and sought it from other men.

She was so special to me, I guess, because a person's first love is usually special, even if that first love is Helga Wark, a perky little cutie meant to go through life putting out for every horny boy who came along.

I remember her as the sexiest and most vivacious teenaged slut Bayporte ever produced.

I imagine that everyone who met her felt pretty much the same way.

The best way to describe Helga would be to say she was Debbie Harry of the rock group Blondie, minus the heroin addiction. Helga had short white-gold hair and prominent cheekbones, as if she'd had her molars extracted. She had big gray eyes that, when she looked at you, made you feel liked and accepted. She also had a beautifully proportioned body and, in the summer, a chocolate-bronze tan.

I loved how Helga could get ready for our dates faster than I could. She wore blouses, skirts and boots, but no makeup or underwear.

"I'm ready!" she'd chirp, pulling a bit of hair away from her eyes.

We'd be off to drink, dance, catch the latest flick or just hang out, with Helga looking hot and trim, ready for a good time, smelling good enough to eat.

She never would have worked out of a place like the Pattison Hotel. No Spandex and stiletto heels for her. She would have sneered at any man who wanted to take her to the back of the room for a ten- or twenty-dollar blow job.

Helga did her thing *her* way.

People called her a "good-time girl" who could outdrink and outdance the men she "dated." She had the ability to manipulate several men at the same time and make each of them think she cared only about him when she hung out at Bayporte's more exclusive places, like the Igloo and Roy's on Royal.

Helga would go there alone, nurse a glass of white wine and figure out who might just be worth her time: upwardly mobile young accountants or conventioneers in town for a few days. They wanted some fun that their wives back home didn't need to know about.

She would zoom in on a guy, pick him up, get a "relationship" going very fast, and pressure him to "lend" her several hundred dollars to get her Miata out of the mechanic's garage. Ultimately, he would not ask for repayment, and she would not offer such.

A few nights later, Helga might appear at a nightclub dressed up but downhearted. Some burglar, she would say as she wiped away tears, had broken into her home and made off with some of her best things, stuff her mum had given her, and for which she had not a dime of insurance.

Within a day or two, the gullible young accountant—"the suit," as she called him—would write her a check for one or two thousand dollars as a "loan" so that she could buy herself some new nice things. He naturally would never see his money again.

Helga, tired of her current benefactor and eager to move on to the next one, could be highly creative in cutting the poor guy loose.

Calling him at the accounting firm or law office that employed him, she would insist that they meet at the Igloo or Roy's on Royal. She had some things they needed to talk about *immediately*.

At the nightclub, as they sipped their cocktails, she would tell him that they needed to call it quits for his "own good."

She would spill it like this: she "sort of" had a "boyfriend" who was one of the "top guns" in one of the city's gangs. Her "fella," a rich, dangerous and jealous man, said he'd kill her if she ever cheated on him. He wanted to see her once a week or so; she shouldn't get too friendly with any of the other men who desired her.

Her gangster, she would reluctantly admit, had treated her well. He paid her credit card bills and rent, but he went on cocaine binges and flew into rages whenever it occurred to him that Helga didn't exactly consider herself his exclusive property. Furthermore, she had made the colossal blunder of telling the suit's name to the gangster.

Now, she fretted, her boyfriend, one of Bayporte's most successful cocaine traffickers and money launderers, admonished her to stop seeing the suit.

"Don't make a fool of me," the gangster had said to the slut. "Don't make a fuckin' fool of me."

"He'll kill you," Helga told the suit.

"He'll do worse than that," said the suit. "He'll destroy my credit rating. He'll tell my boss I'm a closet pedophile. He'll tell my wife I've been screwing you."

The suit would go away, and Helga would tell him that she felt badly about their breakup because, honestly, he had been a much better lay than her gangster.

She kept on with her other suits until she had boffed so many of them so often that they eventually became acquainted with each other and began swapping notes.

"They stopped 'lending' me money, Teddy," she told me later. "I'm like, 'What the fuck?' So I had to go pro. Men can't resist me because I've got to be the sexiest woman in Canada. Which isn't saying much, if you've looked at Canadian women lately."

Helga got smart and rented a gorgeously refurbished three-story house on Heritage Street, near West Shore, the part of Bayporte where all the rich bastards live. The house, while narrow, had a decent-sized back yard surrounded by trees that blocked the neighbors' views of the goings-on.

"Good news," she had told me. "I'm getting top dollars per trick, and I don't declare much on my taxes. It's even more if he chooses to spend the night. I've got a bedroom so great that you would never want to do anything but sleep and screw. Big waterbed and lots of mirrors."

"How come," I asked her, "you keep wanting money from me if business is so good for you?"

"Because," she said, "things get broken around here and need to be replaced. Plus, it gets really slow in the summer, when my clients take off for the States, and we're always running out of pot, poppers, crystal meth and crack."

I felt gratified when, after the failure of her Heritage Street brothel, I gave her a new life when I gave her the money to start her sex website. Helga didn't understand much about her new high-tech venture, so I guess she was doomed from the start, especially since so many other people started doing the same kind of thing, but in Helga's case, naturally everyone who saw her online wanted to meet her in person. She said no, but one man insisted, and she relented.

That man, Tom Kalmar, bursting with money and old enough to be Helga's father, took about fifteen seconds to fall in love with her.

They hurried into their new life together. Tom sent his chain-smoking, alcoholic wife to divorce court and banished his children to Oahu and Australia, where they would spend their lives surfing and living off of monthly checks from Dad. He bought a new wardrobe and a Ferrari, got a haircut and slid a Slayer CD into the car's player.

"Marry me," he said to Helga Wark, "and we'll become Bayporte newest 'hot' couple."

Recently, I stayed put in Bayporte for a couple of months to check on my investments. I attended a party at West Shore Country Club and met up with some of the people who passed for Bayporte's high society. Soon I started to feel that I'd have been better off staying home, pleasuring myself to some Internet porn.

The women gushed about Tom Kalmar's precious new wife, "Helena," and how she was the best thing to happen to Bayporte since anyone could remember.

They went on about how Mrs. Tom Kalmar—the

beautiful, charming and clever Helena—had done a splendid job of renovating their homes in Mexico and Colorado.

I heard about the fine work she had recently done on behalf of the National Organization for Women.

Helena, they said, had become the most driven and dedicated member of the Bayporte Symphony, Variety Club and a half-dozen other charities and philanthropic organizations.

Everybody *wondered* what she ate for breakfast that gave her the energy to do all those things, considering the hours she spent as an adult-literacy volunteer and all her trips to Europe.

By the time Helena arrived at the party, I'd had little enough Canadian Comfort to keep my mouth shut about her former life as Bayporte's town pump.

My ex wore a stunning dark-gray dress and gleaming gold jewelry, she had the skin tone of someone not exactly from the Great White North. Her salon tan looked rich and natural. Dress by Versace, jewelry by Tiffany's. Hair by Sassoon, body by *Playboy*.

I am so happy! her smile said.

Helga, or Helena, or whoever she was now, looked magnificent.

We stood in a small crowd when someone introduced us to each other. Helena told them we were old friends from Oliver Johnson High School. She extended an arm and gave my hand a ladylike squeeze.

"It's so lovely to see you again, Theo."

I tried not to grimace. *Theo?* My birth name was Teddy Leo Crossley. If I'd been inebriated enough, I might have asked her how long she had taken to lose her wrong-side-of-Bayporte accent.

"The crazy people in Mexico throw the *best* parties," Helena told me. "The food in Paris? It's as *exquisite* as you would expect. I can tell you where to dine the next time you're there.

"Have you been to Aspen lately? Frankly, I think Whistler can offer a person a much better time, although it's gotten *terribly* expensive. But getting there is half the fun, and I'm in *love* with our Learjet.

"Bayporte is much more colorful and vibrant than it used to be, don't you think? I'm glad I still live here, now that our city has come into its own.

"You're looking well, Theo, although you may need to shed a few pounds."

I kept waiting for the moment I could tell her to knock off her hoity-toity bullshit, quit calling me Theo and relate to me as one real person to another: Helga Wark to Teddy Crossley. But that moment didn't happen.

Then she updated me on her brothers, some of the worst hoodlums in Bayporte. I would have guessed that at least one was doing time in Rainford or San Quentin for armed robbery and another had become a deadbeat dad pursued by the authorities. Willy was still manning Freddy's Pizza-To-Go and went to an Alcoholics Anonymous meeting every week.

Not so, according to their sister.

"Kelly," she said, "has always been so interested in guns and weapons, became a Canadian Imperial Army officer and he's stationed in Ottawa, consulting the government on the best ways to destroy the enemy.

"Joel is an executive with the Bank of Toronto. He and his wife live in a brownstone in a quaint section of Toronto and they have two *very* lively little ones.

They have season's tickets to the Blue Jays and Maple Leafs.

"Dave and Robby started a security service for Hollywood's elite. I know there was plenty of competition down there for bodyguards and whatnot for the movie stars, but I guess those two boys do that sort of things better than the others because now they're the leading high-end security firm in the Los Angeles area.

"And," she continued, "I know, Theo, that you want to know about your old pal Willy. Well, I know that years ago he was the 'tough guy' of the neighborhood. But that's all changed for him.

"Long story short, he completed his education and then set about educating others. He is now the principal of Oliver Johnson High School."

I didn't see Helga, or Helena, again. I hope I do, and that she's still rich and happy, being Helena the socialite and pretending that Helga the slut has never existed. I admire people who can live their own way and do their own thing.

Bayporte, Great Elizabeth, Canada. My home and native land. Rain, skyscrapers, mountains, Starbucks. The mighty Tyson River dividing the city in half. A city that doesn't know how unsophisticated it is. Not an hour away, a Canadian Imperial Army base sends soldiers off to Kabul. Near Bayporte's West Shore, in Northup University's football stadium, fans cheer "Thrash 'em!" as the Northup Kodiaks take on the visiting team. I'm proud to say I went to Northup on scholarship, played golf there for four years and graduated with a degree in something or other. Northup University may be the only Canadian college people in other countries have heard of.

My dad, during my childhood, had gone to Montreal because he wanted to be far from Bayporte, and soon later my mum went up to the Yukon. That left my uncles, aunts and a grandmother to provide whatever supervision I needed. They told me that my dad was a very decent man who had simply fallen out of love with my mum. She moved to the Yukon because my dad had gone away. I was OK, because my uncles, aunts and I laughed all the time. I wouldn't have traded my life for anybody's in West Shore, or

Beverly Hills, or anywhere else. I knew many people left Bayporte for reasons they left unsaid. Maybe the rain did it to them.

My mum wrote me to say that the Yukon was better because the people were warmer and friendlier, if only to compensate for the coldness and desolation of the terrain. She added that I would probably enjoy meeting Detlev, who worked as an ice pilot, if I ever went up there to visit.

My dad wrote me from Montreal and said that even the Frenchies who spoke English pretended they didn't. He told me he felt glad to see that the Northup Kodiaks football team had gone undefeated, and he didn't think the Habs would ever win another Stanley Cup. He said I should go out there some day and see him. I would probably like Lally, because she liked golf.

I played golf because I couldn't play hockey. On the floor or ice, I couldn't move fast enough or hit hard enough. We had an old set of golf clubs in our garage, and my uncle, watching me try out those clubs, said that I had a good swing and should take it up as a hobby.

Golf, he said, was a different kind of game. You could play it your whole life, and it didn't destroy your body the way other games did. What's more, golf would keep you outdoors and you could meet people who had lots of money. If you got good enough, you could spend the rest of your life playing golf. It would beat the hell out of working for a living.

For my birthday, I'm not sure which one, my uncle gave me his Taylormade clubs. Even now I consider that the best birthday I'd ever had and the best gift. I've used other woods since then, naturally, but I still love those old irons, which have been through more restorative surgery than an aging movie star.

I've tried all the brands by now—Ping, Nike, Titleist, Mizuno—but I keep going back to my uncle's old Taylormades, the way an older woman at a dance will keep grooving with the youngster who brought her there.

When I make it to the big tournaments, like the Open here in Bayporte, I think back to my younger days at Beaver Hills, when at fifteen I had everyone treating me like an adult. I've lost touch with most of those guys, some or most of whom are surely now dead, but whenever I've gotten further professionally than anyone would have guessed, I always say to my Beaver Hills gang, under my breath,

"Wish me luck, fellas."

HOLE IN ONE

PART 4:
THE BIG
ENCHILADA

HOLE IN ONE

6

On Sunday morning at the Hotel Bayporte, I awoke with a hangover and could barely tolerate the TV pitchman who wanted to sell me household gadgets at Depression-era prices. My head felt on fire and my mouth tasted foul, so I did the only logical thing: I lit up a Player's Light.

Nancy, fully dressed, sat on the sofa at the other end of the suite. Her suitcases bulged at her feet.

I looked at the wall clock and saw that I still had plenty of time to recover from the previous night's boozing and make it to the golf course. If I lost the Open, it wouldn't be because of being tardy or absent.

"I need java," I muttered, clearing my throat.

Nancy pointed at the room service cart in the middle of the suite. She loved to talk, so her gesture meant she wanted to punish me. Naturally vivacious, and fond of me most of the time, she would be as uncomfortable with her meanness as I was.

I stumbled to the cart and checked it out. "What? No sugar or cream, eh?"

"Guess not," Nancy murmured, staring at the TV set.

I grunted and called room service for a fresh pot. In the meantime, I smoked some more and tried not to think about golf.

"Canadian Comfort over ice," I said, "sure is nice."

Nancy made a tiny sound in spite of herself.

"Have we met?" I asked her. "My name's Teddy Crossley, and I'm here to compete in the Canadian Open."

She said nothing for several moments, then broke her silence. "We have things we need to talk about."

I frowned. "Did you throw all my clothes out the window?"

A year or so earlier, at the South Florida Open in

Fort Lauderdale, something happened that Nancy found humiliating.

We had gone to a party down there that I had an obligation to attend. This particular event happened in an old, renovated mansion someone had rented. Barbecued steaks sizzled in the back yard, a bar stood every twenty feet and a hundred or more guests milled about.

Such parties attract an eclectic crowd. Tiger wasn't there, but I saw John Daly and Jack Nicklaus, and a number of golfers of my stature had shown up. TV stars, smooth-talking sportscasters, corporate men sweating in suits, ad agency hotshots and Nike and Ping sales reps were easy to spot.

So were the wives, girlfriends and prostitutes.

For most of the party, we hung back and looked around with Harold Baumer. Nancy smirked at the number of men in pink jackets, plaid pants and white shoes.

"You sure you want to go to this thing?" I had asked her. "This will be your first big golf party. It'll be full of drunken, lecherous men, you know, even worse than me."

"I used to *sing* for drunken men five nights a week. They don't scare me."

Unfortunately, at that party, Nancy, a properly endowed Canadian lass, looked not unlike some of the Chrissies or Cassies whom our hosts hired to get friendly with the men who could afford that kind of entertainment.

The hookers took the men to the upstairs bedrooms and were admonished to be most discreet about it. But between trysts, which lasted maybe half an hour, the ladies would come downstairs and mingle some more, sipping 7-Up and casing the house for valuable stuff not nailed down.

Nancy soon got miffed because the steak they served her in the back yard had too much gristle and fat. Plus, they had no HP sauce or Canada Dry ginger ale, her favorite kind of pop.

A provocatively dressed young woman sauntered up to Nancy.

"Is this your first party, hon? I haven't seen you around. Do you work the clubs or the strolls?"

I remember thinking, *Well, that's Southern women for you. If you have a good body, you must be making a living off of it.*

"Not me, sweetie," Nancy said. "I'm not a player, I'm just a wife."

The pross gave her a little smile and sashayed off to say hi to a group of Northeasterners who had been ogling her goodies.

Not two minutes later, some disheveled guy hustled by and grabbed Nancy by the hand. "Wanna be my friend?" he asked as he pulled her towards the staircase.

He pulled some more, and she went along. I even waved goodbye, thinking that they were just having a bit of fun and, if he tried anything, Nancy would straighten his ass out good. I turned to Harold Baumer and resumed our golf talk.

Nancy stayed upstairs a bit longer than expected. I guessed she was really cussing him out. Harold and I were asking each other if we should go upstairs and save the poor *schnook* from my crazy Canadian wife, when she came bounding down the stairs, red-faced and shaking with rage.

Nancy marched right past us, giving her dress a little tug as she left the way we had come.

"Fuckin' *goof*," was all she said.

A man had followed her down the stairs. Not the one who had pulled her by the hand. This guy seemed mentally together.

"I'm sorry, Ted," he said to me. "We didn't know who she was, and that dude was so drunk…"

Later, back in our hotel room, Nancy said, "That drunk? He pulled me into a bedroom and locked the door. Then he threw a hundred-dollar bill onto the dresser and said. 'This is for lookin' so good.'

"I told him, 'Look, you have the wrong idea. I'm not a whore. I'm a wife. You want a whore? There's plenty of them downstairs.' He didn't say anything, he just got naked and started talking dirty, like, 'Oh, yeah, them titties, I gotta have them big juicy titties..' He lunged at my chest and I pushed him away.

"Well, he got behind me and poked his hard-on into my bum. He said, 'Take off your dress and stay awhile.' He kissed my neck and said, 'Do you know any black chicks? Have you ever made it with a black chick? I'd be down for *that*, baby.'

"I slapped his hands away and got out of there, fast. He was right behind me, pumpin' his thing and saying, 'Do me, do me, do me.' In the hallway, this other guy, not drunk at all, came out from a different room, and the drunk started singing, 'Black and white, ebony and ivory, chocolate and vanilla…' He sort of collapsed against the wall and kept laughing, and the sober guy said, 'You idiot! She's not a hooker! She's a golfer's wife!'"

I shrugged at her retelling of the incident. "Like I said, lots of golfers, lots of booze. Shit happens."

She snarled. "I'm glad *you* think it's a laughing fuckin' matter."

The following morning, I awoke to discover that much of my wardrobe had disappeared. After a few minutes of searching, I looked out the window and found out that my clothes were on the lawn outside our hotel room. As I pulled on my sweatpants and T-shirt to retrieve my sportscoats and slacks, Nancy emerged from the washroom.

"You're lucky I just threw them out instead of cutting them up," she told me. "If I had cut them up, I would have cut off other things, too. You wouldn't have missed it, though. All you use it for is peeing."

That experience soured me on Fort Lauderdale, but I have long felt a deep fondness for Augusta, home of the Masters, and I suppose that every pro golfer loves that place. The course itself is gorgeous, yet it's also fun and fair to play on.

"It's prestigious and elite as all hell," I told Bronwen, who went with me my first time there. "There are a few ways of getting into the Masters, but you must win one tournament or another beforehand. Since it's very difficult to win anything in this business, the field of eligible players is only a fraction of what it is for other tournaments."

I got into the Masters by winning the Ottawa Open, which is not such a big deal. On our way to Georgia, I played in South Carolina. As we drove to the Masters, I told Bronwen what we should expect.

"There'll be flowers everywhere—azaleas, dogwoods, whatever else," I said. "Dixie at this time of year is something to see.

"From the veranda, you can see the course itself, and it's greener than emeralds. You can see the leaderboard and the housing that they built for presidents and other V.I.P.s

"In the clubhouse, of course, everyone is close to whispering. That's the way they behave in that environment. Lots of old white men in green jackets, azaleas everywhere, everyone speaking in a soothing whisper. So much tradition, and all those smug Southerners who want to keep things just as they are."

I laughed. "Then came Tiger Woods, winning the thing for the first time at twenty-one. A tall, skinny black kid from California wearing that green jacket in that old white boys' club. Who woulda thunk?"

I sighed. "I could probably spend all day in the Trophy Room, from what I've heard about it. Just looking at those great old golf clubs that the champs have used. While we're at Augusta, we might also have a piece of that peach pie they talk so much about. Sounds good, hey?"

When I steered the car onto the Augusta grounds that very first time, I felt as exhilarated and awed as a little boy at Disneyland. But instead of seeing flags and balloons and a giant Mickey Mouse, I beheld a long avenue of magnolias leading up to the clubhouse.

"Paradise!" I gushed to Bronwen. "The elite. The best of the best. They've all driven up here to be a part of this. And now we're here."

"Let me out," she said. "I've got to do number one. Do you think they'd mind if I peed in the magnolias?"

A bit later on, I suggested that she try to make friends with the other wives. When we approached some of them in the clubhouse, the wives, all reasonably young, were tapping on iPads or chatting on iPhones. They seemed scarcely aware of each other, much less us.

"Hey, gang!" Bronwen called out with false cheer. "I'm Bronnie. Wanna be my friend?"

I excused myself and went to hit some balls. When I came back, Bronwen told me about her visit with the other wives.

"Mostly," she said, "they bitched about how much their pediatricians charged them, which of the Southern Hiltons had the best weekend packages, and how difficult it could be to get a spending-limit increase on their American Express cards."

"So you gave them a bit of backtalk, eh? You were being a smartmouth. That doesn't go over very well around here. They really admire good manners."

Bronwen wiped away an imaginary tear. "Then I guess I just won't ever fit in at the Masters."

Nancy turned towards me as she sat on the sofa in our suite at the Hotel Bayporte.

"You," she said, "are a very bad person. You pay no attention to me, so whatever I may have done with Troy Frisby was more your fault than mine.

"But there's something else you need to know. Troy and I are in love. We are going to Vegas or somewhere and get married just as soon as Troy and Andrea see their lawyer and figure out what's what.

"Troy and me? It was just a sexual thing at first. Don't you think he looks like Don Johnson, only taller? But we have fallen deeply and hopelessly in love, mainly because *you* were never around to provide the love that I needed.

"You may get your jollies by swinging a stick at a ball, but *I* need more than that."

"Nancy," I said, "thank you for your candor and openness. I don't know how else to say this, so I'll be blunt: If you think Troy Frisby is going to divorce Andrea and marry you, one of us is a fuckin' fool. Troy Frisby is so stingy that he would never go through a divorce even if Andrea paid *him* alimony. He'll stay with her just for financial reasons."

"You don't know him like I do," Nancy retorted.

"I know him far better than you ever will. He will never break up his marriage."

"It's already broken up," she said.

"Really? Who told you that?"

"Andrea Frisby. She knows about us."

"Oh." Somehow, I didn't expect that.

"Andrea took it well. She said she knew he'd played around a lot. She also noticed how much I talked about him and always tried to sit next to him. She asked Troy if I was the one he really wanted, and he said yes."

"What he said is meaningless. He lies all the time and changes his mind every fifteen minutes."

Nancy put her hands on her hips. "*You* just don't understand about love. You don't know how it feels to touch and be touched, to feel the *ecstasy* of it all."

"Like fuck I don't. I feel the *ecstasy* every time I'm out on the course and I make a good shot. It's as satisfying to me as coming with a woman. I'm coming for eighteen holes, with everybody watching. Sometimes it's embarrassing." Then, "Well, thank you for telling me all this, instead of just leaving me a 'Dear Teddy' note on the dresser and buggering off with Troy."

"We felt you were entitled to an explanation. We thought you might already know what was going on. Andrea might have told Bronwen and Bronwen might have told you."

I shook my head. "Bronwen wouldn't do that. She can keep secrets as well as anyone I've ever met."

I then felt so sorry for Nancy. Married to me but in love with a slick hustler like Troy, she was far too dumb to emerge from this mess as any kind of winner.

I pointed to her zippered, bulging suitcases. "Where are you going?"

"To be with Troy. We're going to the Midwest where they're having a couple of tournaments. I'm going to watch the rest of the Open on the TV. I hope Troy kicks your ass. I think he will, because you always choke under pressure."

"Here's the deal," I said to her. "I don't want our separation to get ugly. If it's about money, I'll give you whatever is fair."

"The lawyers will figure *that* out."

"Just remind the lawyers not to shake me down too hard, or I might have to show them a little movie I have on my computer: 'The Golfer's Cheating Wife,' starring Nancy Crossley."

"In the meantime," she said, "I need some pocket money."

I took out my wallet and handed over most of my one thousand dollars in cash. "If you want to go back to our apartment, go ahead. I won't be there. I may get a hotel room near the hospital and visit Bronwen every day." I added, "There's plenty in our checking account, and I know you have every credit card known to humankind. I don't imagine we'll be seeing each other again for a while—or ever. But I wouldn't want you to feel inconvenienced out there in that hard world."

"I've felt 'inconvenienced' ever since we got married. Now I'm making things more 'convenient' for myself."

She phoned downstairs and asked for bell service.

"I better get a shave and go to the golf course." As I headed towards the washroom, I turned to her and said, as she hung up the phone, "No hard feelings, eh? Nancy, I have enjoyed our time together and I hope things work out between you and Troy, if that's what you want."

Then I took one last lingering look at Nancy's gravity-defying breasts and went in to shower.

At the Placid Oaks clubhouse, I spent some time in the private room for players and "official personnel." Troy and I were scheduled to play that afternoon, so I had several hours in which to drink many cups of coffee, read the headlines on my iPad and take a number of prolonged pisses.

Then, just for fun, I used the memo function on my iPad to compose a document:

TEDDY CROSSLEY'S CURRENT GRIEVANCES

1. The Grim Reaper has a death grip on Bronwen.
2. I'm pretty sure I'm going to choke here at the Canadian Open.
3. I hate myself, and that's not altogether a good thing.
4. Troy Frisby is considered a modern Canadian hero.
5. I am homeless.
6. By now, Nancy has probably looted our checking account.
7. I am well into my 30s and have dick to show for it.
8. Helga Wark has become a Bayporte socialite.
9. I will have to drive to Manitoba for my next tournament.
10. If I choke today and blow my lead, I will become the laughingstock of Canada and may have to find another career (if, in fact, one can call what I'm doing now a "career").
11. For the past couple of days, I have been

constipated.

12. Willy Wark has become a successful man.

13. I am hungry but cannot think of anything good to eat.

14. If I don't quit smoking Player's Lights soon, I will probably end up like Bronwen.

15. The Bayporte wind is probably going to blow my shots into the wilderness and cost me my first-ever Canadian National Open Title.

16. I've used up all my Tylenol 3s.

17. I'm homeless and constipated. Life's so unfair.

18. If I win this Open, some very annoying people are going to insist on buying me a drink.

19. American Express will soon start saying, "Your authorization has been declined."

20. I didn't try hard enough to make things work out with Bronwen.

21. God is laughing His ass off at me.

Harold came by with lunch for me: a fruit salad and

a glass of unsweetened iced tea.

"Don't think about the Open right now," he said.

"Oh? And what should I think about?"

"Did I tell you I'm looking for new clubs? Irons, mostly."

"Did Troy tell you to do that?"

"No, it's my own idea. I'm thinking of playing a lot of tournaments in the States in the next few months. Maybe I should get those new irons just for that.

"You're still going to Europe next month, right, Teddy? Maybe I'll do that, too. I want to have the experience in playing overseas."

"Don't ask me a bunch of questions right now, Harold. I can't think straight. I just need to get through these next few hours. I've got Bronwen on the brain, too. Can't really concentrate on anything else." Then, "I guess you know about Nancy and me."

He pouted. "Too bad, eh?"

I nodded and pushed my iPad towards him. He read up on my grievances.

"Constipation," I muttered.

"That's good. It shows you care."

"Constipation," I said, "is not good, Harold."

7

At just before one, I decided to get dressed and get busy. I put on my black golf shirt, gray slacks and cleats. I put a few new pairs of black gloves into my pockets and went outside. My caddy, Giberson, stood outside the clubhouse with my clubs.

"Let's go get you warmed up," he said.

I nodded and we went to the practice area, where I hit several dozen balls and took my time about it. Over at the putting green, I tapped on the balls just hard enough for them to enter a green machine that immediately spat the balls back at me.

I stood there for a minute or two and looked around at the gloriousness of Placid Oaks. I saw people sipping cocktails on the veranda of the modern, gleaming-white clubhouse. I looked up at the lead-gray sky and saw the Canadian flag flapping in the wind, the flag of the province of Great Elizabeth below it and the CPGA flag at the bottom.

Wow, I said to myself. I still can't believe I'm here at Placid Oaks. I'm only half an hour away from Beaver Hills, yet this is another world.

I looked all around me, at the immaculate white tents and the countless people who'd come out to see their Canadian boys, Teddy Crossley and Troy Frisby, win this Canadian Open for the Great White North.

Also, of course, they had come to check out the most famous and successful golf player of the past two decades.

"Fuckin' Tiger," I said aloud, reading the leaderboard. "He's catching up with me. He's birdied almost everything so far today. Unreal."

"He won't get to you if you forget about him and just play good golf," Giberson said.

As I stood still and tortured myself with visions of a Tiger clawback, I heard cheers and applause from far away on the course.

"Fuckin' Tiger's just birdied again," I muttered. "He's two strokes back of me, and I haven't even started." Could fuckin' Tiger shoot a 63? Nobody had ever done that well at Placid Oaks.

The main thing was that the Open had become a

three-man contest: Tiger, Troy and me. Naturally, I had to play my very best just to beat Troy, to say nothing of holding off the fabled and legendary fuckin' Tiger. Did the crowd here, and those watching elsewhere in Canada, *really* want one of their own to win this time, or would they feel gratified to see you-know-who take over another major tournament?

Harold bounded up towards me, all smiles and chuckles.

"That bloody Tiger is starting to roar," he said.

"Fuckin' Tiger," I retorted, smiling as my putt went nice and straight.

"His birdies are just flukes," Harold said. "He can't keep it up for much longer. He doesn't know Placid Oaks well enough."

I hit a couple more practice putts and smiled again.

"Teddy," said Giberson, "it's getting to be that time."

Harold shook my hand.

"Don't let me down," he said.

"Or myself," I muttered.

"Gibby," I said to my caddy, "would you go into the clubhouse and get me a pack of Player's Lights and something to drink."

"What kind of drink?" he asked.

"Anything—beer, wine, pop—as long as it's nice and cold."

"Gotcha."

As soon as he left, Andrea appeared.

"Troy's not around," I said to her. "Did he quit or something?"

She shook her head. "He arrived before you did. He's done his putting practice, and now he's out at the first tee."

"Hey, I'm sorry about you and Troy and all this ugliness. Nancy told me what's been going on. I hope you haven't been too traumatized by this whole thing."

Andrea shrugged. "Oh, I'm fine."

"Nancy," I said, "seems to think that Troy is leaving you to marry her. Does she speak the truth?"

"Well, he and I are calling it quits. I'm tired of him and his playing around. But Nancy? She's not his only girlfriend, no matter what he told her."

Giberson came up to us and said, "Gots to do that thang, Teddy."

"Ted," Andrea said as we walked along, "Tiger might beat Troy but I don't think he'll catch up with *you*."

I kissed her on the forehead and disappeared into the crowd. When I ducked under the gallery rope and went to the tee, I heard robust applause.

Troy stood before me, jiving and shucking in his rainbow-striped shirt and burnt-orange slacks. Next to him were several Open officials in blazers, striped ties and oxford slacks.

The officials all shook my hands. Troy and I exchanged unsmiling nods.

I put on a new glove. Giberson handed me a ball and tee.

"I'm using Nikes," Troy said.

"I've got Pings," I said.

We stood there for the longest time, looking in each other's direction and staying silent.

"I think," Tory murmured, "we're supposed to kiss and rub noses or something."

"You know what you can kiss," I retorted as I

stepped away to have a good look at our first fairway.

It seemed that most of Bayporte had shown up for this event. Behind the ropes, humanity stretched on forever. I saw, in the distance, a guy waving a flagstick at us, alerting the bosses that the golfers in front of us had finished playing and we were OK to tee off.

I sighed and pulled on my glove a bit.

One of the officials, appealing for silence, raised his hands at the fans crowded behind the ropes. After a few minutes, everyone grew silent.

"Fore, please," the official said.

The grounds had grown so quiet that we could hear the clinking of cocktail glasses from the clubhouse behind us.

"This," the official said, "is the two-oh-five starting time for the fourth and final round of the Open Championship of the Canadian Professional Golfers' Association. On the tee, Troy C. Frisby"—he rattled off Troy's scores, which were quite good, and I had to admire Troy for being so loose and cool, while I wanted to vomit and defecate—"and Teddy Leo Crossley"—he gave my scores, too.

I nodded as the crowd showered us with their

applause. I also felt relieved that Mother Nature had chosen to keep us, and the greens, dry.

The official went up to Troy and said, "Mister Frisby, I believe it's your honor."

The official backed up and said, "Gentlemen, play away."

Troy hammered his tee ball so well that, if nobody had been watching, I would have paid him to hit mine, too. His ball sailed past the cluster of oaks and came to rest on the edge of the green. Nice. If he kept that up, he would have his ball in the cup with two more strokes, meaning three in total, which would be great, because this hole at Placid Oaks was a par five.

He knew he'd made a good shot, so he chuckled and did a little dance as he returned his club to his caddy. He turned to the spectators and took a bow.

"Thought for a minute I would have a hole in one," he told them.

For fuck's sake, I thought, now he's going to be Mr. Funny Guy, and I'll have to wait for them to shut up before I can tee off.

Despite feeling quite uncomfortable due to the crowds and TV cameras, plus the few oversized, rock-hard stools sitting in my bowels, I stepped up, took a swing and made a very respectable shot myself.

I hurried down the middle of the fairway and tried to find the tiny speck of white that was my golf ball.

"I don't know who's going to win this thing," I said to Giberson as he tried to keep up with me, "but if he wants to learn about golf hustling, I'll be happy to take him to Beaver Hills."

"Beaver Hills?" Giberson asked, panting. "Where is that? Never heard of it."

"It's where I learned about life and became a man," I said.

Troy, damn his ass, birdied that hole but I did not. I used a one-iron and got my ball onto the green in two strokes. But then I hit the ball too hard and it sped right past the hole by at least thirty feet. No way in hell could I make a thirty-footer.

I got the ball as close as five feet to the cup, a putt I could usually make in my sleep. But this time the ball rolled around the cup and then danced away.

"That one," confided Giberson, "has a mind of its

own, and it's decided it doesn't like you."

I looked up at the cloudy but rainless Bayporte sky and addressed the Big Golfer in the Sky.

"Yeah," I said sotto voce, "it's Teddy again, and I wish You would cut me some slack down here."

Our next few holes were scarcely as challenging. Troy made two birdies and caught up with me. When I checked the leaderboard, it said that Tiger Woods was only a couple of strokes back.

Troy and I refused to speak to each other.

But then, on the sixth tee, he started trying to mess with my head. Just as I got ready to whack the fuck out of the ball with my iron, he cleared his throat.

Loudly.

I couldn't *see* it, of course, but I could hear it, and it upset my rhythm a tiny bit, and Troy should have known better than to do such a thing. My shot went off all right anyway, but still.

As we marched towards the green, I looked around to see if anyone might be within earshot.

"Hey, douche bag," I said. "Don't be doing dumbass things while I'm hitting the ball. You hear me?"

Troy frowned. "Hey?"

"You cleared your throat just as I swung at the ball. I'm just lucky I didn't end up in the rough or miss the ball completely."

He shrugged. "Sorry about that. Won't happen again."

"You just wait till you have to make a big putt. I'm gonna fart loud enough to wake the dead."

Troy putted first on the next hole and ended up just a couple of feet from the cup. Instead of tapping it in, he marked his ball with a quarter and stepped aside as I prepared to putt for a birdie.

"I can't make this putt," I muttered to Giberson.

"Whatcha gonna do?" he asked.

"I'll waste Troy's time and drive him nuts."

I did just that. I walked all around the ball, squatting and staring, removing little bits of nothing from around the path connecting my ball to the cup.

Giberson and I stood side by side, talking about every break my ball might take. I asked a couple of photographers to back off a bit. I cocked my head up and looked skyward, as if a bird were about to shit on me. Finally, I caught a glimpse of Troy a few dozen steps away, fidgeting with his golf bag.

I stepped back from my ball, checked it out, backed up even more, looked at it some more. At last I tried to tap it home.

It went to the lip of the cup and stayed there.

"Shit," I said, then stared at the ball with my meanest glower, hoping it would get intimidated and drop into the hole to placate me.

"Asshole, fuckstick," I muttered, giving my ball the gentlest tap and watching it go in. I made sure I stepped on Troy's quarter as I went away and he came in.

"Hey, guy," he said, "you stepped on my coin."

"I'm so sorry. Gee, I'll never forgive myself if you miss your putt."

Giberson and I started off towards the next tee. As we moved past the spectators, I heard loud moans and groans. Troy, it seemed, had missed his easy little putt.

Our next few holes were largely unmemorable. I made a poor drive that would have gone into the rough, but the wind straightened it out and I ended up in reasonably good shape. Troy ended up in a sand trap but made a great shot to get out of the sand and onto the green.

Giberson and I walked to the ninth hole with me a stroke ahead of Troy and two on Tiger. I'd heard no happy noises from Tiger's party so I guessed he hadn't done anything phenomenal or miraculous in the last little while. He would be at the 16th hole or near it.

As I teed up on the ninth hole, something attracted my attention. Troy started teeing up, too. I was supposed to go first, because he had gone over par on the hole before this one.

"Troy, dear," I said, "would you bugger off for a bit?"

Some fans overheard me and laughed. Troy made a face, pulled up his tee and stepped aside.

This, the ninth hole, is one of Placid Oaks' easiest: wide open, with none of the trees, sand traps, lakes or other nuisances that make many players fear and loathe this course. Smirking, I spoke to the ball and made sure I was loud enough for the closest spectators to over hear me.

"Go straight home for Daddy. You know where home is. Daddy wants you to go home and wait there till he picks you up."

The ball, once airborne, looked as if it wanted to say, *There's no intelligent life down there, Daddy. I think I'll stay up here for a while.*

The crowd whistled, hollered and cheered. I heard Harold's voice above the din.

"Go baby! Oh baby! Yeah baby! Awright!"

The nice people cheered me on to the next fairway, even though I hadn't played remarkable well and barely maintained my lead. Still, I had the lead.

But as I got nearer to the green that was closest to the clubhouse, nodding and smiling at the many people waving at me, I heard a roar very similar to the one I expected when I sank my last putt and became the first Canadian winner of the Canadian National Open since who knew when.

This roar scared me. It scared Giberson, too.

"He did something," Giberson said. "Something

big."

Fuckin' Tiger.

"He eagled the sixteenth, I'll bet." I snarled.

Troy rushed up to Giberson and me.

"Do you think," he asked, "that Tiger can shoot eagles from here on out?"

"Do *you* think," I retorted, "that we can get a hit man out here to take care of him before that happens?"

Troy said, "If he keeps up this shit, he's going to be waving that fuckin' trophy around while we're still driving and putting."

Giberson handed me a white towel and I wiped my face and neck.

"No," I said to Giberson and Troy. "He hasn't won *yet*. He hasn't won anything *yet*. Right?"

We went inside the clubhouse and looked at the leaderboard, which would change in a moment. It did, and now read:

T. Woods, eagle three, 16th.

Tiger, seven under par for the round now, could easily finish with a score in the low 60s. Jack Nicklaus, another American golf icon, had set the record, 63, at

Placid Oaks years earlier.

The moment Tiger's score went up on the board, most of our cheering section went buggering off to check him out.

"Ingrates," I muttered. "What kind of Canadians are you? Want some pampered brat from Stanford to beat *me*?"

"Teddy," said Giberson, "don't take this so personally. These people are just starstruck. I mean, it's not every day that Tiger Woods comes to town."

"Yeah," I said, "and it's not every day that Tiger Woods plays a major tournament in Canada against a Canadian."

"*Two* Canadians," Troy said.

"And then they start cheering for Tiger. Unreal."

"Are we on the air yet?" Troy asked. "Tiger may wrap this up even before the red light goes on."

"Don't worry about it," I said. "They'll have it all on tape. So will the fans. They come here with their cell phones and Camcorders and see all kinds of shit that's supposed to be private."

Troy frowned at me, and I at him.

"Teddy," he said, "we need to talk about some

things after the Open is over. I'm not the bad guy in this little drama, no matter what you think. I did screw Nancy, but she was really the aggressor—"

"Who cares?"

"I just want you to know how it is," he said.

"I already do. You're just trying to put your own spin on it."

"I wouldn't have done it," he told me, "if I thought you two were happy and in love."

"That right, eh?"

"You and I have been friends for years. I wouldn't lie to you."

"But you *would* fuck my old lady." I shook my head and chuckled. "I can't believe I'm talking about this while I'm standing here in Placid Oaks, leading in the Canadian Open."

"Teddy, she made the first move. She said you two were splitsville. Otherwise, I wouldn't have touched her. I don't do that kind of thing to my friends."

"You must take a great deal of comfort in talking like that and thinking like that," I said.

"I'm just trying to be straight up and totally honest with you."

"Thank you for your candor," I said. "Now you go on to the next tournament and diddle Nancy while I try to diddle Tiger here."

We were just finishing the first half of the Open and made par but not much else. We started the back nine as if we'd suddenly forgotten everything we had ever learned about the fundamentals of golf.

I ended up a few times in the trees, managed to get onto the green and missed a couple of no-brainer putts. I made par on those three holes. Troy, however, began communing with nature—trees, sand and water—and fell to three strokes behind me as we began the 13th hole. He could not win now.

Giberson's cell phone rang. He answered it, spoke a bit, listened a bit, then put it away.

"Teddy," he said, smiling, "that was from someone following Tiger. *He* just *bogeyed* the seventeenth!"

"Tiger bogeyed it? For real?"

Giberson nodded. "Three-putted it. Parred the eighteenth. Finished up with a two-seventy-nine."

I had a one-shot lead on Tiger Woods with six holes left. If I made par on each of them, I would win by one stroke. If I bogeyed one, I would tie him, but screw that. I didn't want to play any tiebreaker against Mistah Woods.

At the 13th, we had to wait while someone up ahead took a dump or something. Troy sat next to me on a bench inside the ropes while the officials stood nearby.

The bosses acknowledged us because, for the moment, I had the lead. The sports reporters, too, had narrowed it down to me and Tiger, and as soon as one of us won the damn thing, they would move in with their questions.

I felt stupid, sitting there next to a man I had known for a long time and just ignoring him. So I looked in his direction.

"Andrea is a damn fine woman," I said. "Bad idea to go eat hamburger when you have filet mignon at home."

"You know the hamburger better than I do," he conceded, looking at the ground around my feet. "Maybe you're right about Nancy. I know you're right about Andrea. But I don't know if I want to try saving my marriage. We have no kids, and that makes everything very convenient." He paused. "They say that if you're married, you shouldn't fuck around, and that if you want to fuck around, you shouldn't be married. Well, I guess I should just keep fucking around and never remarry."

I lit up a Player's Light and thought for a bit about what he had just said.

"Andrea," I said, "knows much more than you suspect about all your girlfriends scattered far and wide."

Troy nodded.

"She's one hell of a woman," I said. "Very special."

"That's the trouble," he said. "They're *all* special."

Over the next several holes I ended up in the trees once or twice and in the sand, too. Somehow I got myself out of each mess; Giberson would hand me a club, I would take my best whack at the ball and God would do the rest.

Honestly, I made pars despite myself. On the 13th, I took a dreadful swing at the ball but it somehow ended up on the green. At the next hole, I sliced my shot so badly that it appeared to head straight for the water, but it smacked some guy in the head instead and landed on the green.

On the 15th, stupefied by exhaustion, I putted the damn ball in the general direction of the cup. But the ball hit a cleat mark, followed a groove I hadn't read, and dropped in.

On my tee shot at hole 17, I got carried away and put far too much body English into my swing. My ball sailed so far off into the woods that I feared we would have to send in the search-and-rescue boys. But once I located it, I discovered a huge clearing in the trees.

Miraculously, I traipsed onto the 18th tee still holding a one-shot lead over Tiger. I still had to wait because of the vast numbers of people and their reluctance to obey the security personnel.

As I looked down the fairway, I could see nothing but people, and I reminded me of pictures I had seen of Woodstock, the 1969 rock concert. Somewhere out there, unseen by me, sat the last hole, where this whole ordeal would end.

Everyone had something to say to me, but their

voices all blended into some kind of weird music I ignored.

"You can do this, Teddy," said Troy. "Do it to him. Don't get lazy. Kick Tiger's ass."

"No worries here," said Giberson, handing me an iron. "We own Tiger. We have him all caged up. Canada's going to give the trophy to one of her own this year."

Harold stood at the ropes, just a few feet away.

"That Tiger's through, Teddy," Harold said. "It's yours to win. Go get it."

"It's like I said," Grover told him, "Tiger's in the cage. He's all locked up."

I did what I was supposed to do. I teed off, but I didn't feel the impact of the driver striking the ball. Still, the ball sailed through the air and made it onto the green. My head felt full of white noise as I walked with Giberson towards my ball.

I thought of my current opponent, Eldrick Tont "Tiger" Woods, who had played golf since learning to walk, so who could be surprised by his professional success? I didn't know him well, but I wondered how, deep down inside, he felt about having devoted his entire life to this dumbass game.

"I would like," I told Giberson, "to be able to win this Open with a one-foot putt."

"Well," he said, smiling, "I think you've got a pretty good chance of winning it, no matter what happens."

I forced myself not to think about the shot. I just did it: I swung the club and hit the ball. It felt right. It looked right, too. Sometimes, the ball just knows where Daddy wants it to go.

I clapped my caddy on the back and laughed.

"Gibby," I said, "I think we got that fuckin' Tiger just where he want him."

I believe that even a legless man would have enjoyed walking down that last fairway, his head full of cheers and applause from vast numbers of spectators.

My ball sat only a dozen feet from the cup. Even Stevie Wonder could have sunk it in two taps. I putted it straight at the cup, the ball died just inches from victory, and instead of making the world wait for my win, I tapped it again and won the Canadian Open.

The crowd went berserk, and Giberson threw his arms around me. Then Troy jumped on the two of us. Harold ducked under the ropes to join our love fest.

The bunch of us tumbled to the ground, so I didn't get a chance to throw my ball into the crowd or do some arm-pumping poses for the photographers.

When the chaos had died down a bit in our little celebratory scene, I looked over and saw Tiger by the scorer's tent, visiting with some officials. He smiled and waved at me.

I bounded over to him and shook his hand.

"Tiger," I said, "you better watch out. If I win just twenty more majors, I'll almost be tied with you."

Each person celebrates his best days in his own way. If your name is Tiger Woods, and you've won nearly two dozen big golf tournaments and you're not yet 40, you've already had many celebrations. So you go out for an insanely expensive dinner at the best restaurant in whichever city you're in. You eat the best dish on the menu, drink their best wine and pay the check with your American Express black card.

But, of course, there is only one Tiger Woods. If you happen to be Teddy Leo Crossley, you go back to your hotel with Harold Baumer and get gooned on Canadian Comfort over ice. You talk and laugh about the Open and neither of you can quite believe that Teddy has actually *won* the damn thing. Especially Teddy.

"That was the first time I'd ever held the trophy," I said, sipping my drink. "It felt light and phony, like plastic. Seemed like a ripoff."

"They say it's worth two thousand bucks, but they lie." Harold laughed. "You should put the fucker on eBay and see how much you can get."

We drank a toast to every Canadian golfer we could think of, which took about fifteen seconds, and then we toasted the famous golfers, which took somewhat longer.

"This trophy," Harold said, "isn't even the original Canadian Open trophy. They broke it or lost it some years ago, so they had a new one made up. Doesn't matter. It's just something they give you to hold up and kiss while they take your picture."

"Well," I said, making no effort to stifle a huge belch, "I don't give a fuck *what* it's made of. It means that I won the Open and that's that."

We drank some more, sang some stupid songs and then Harold fell asleep on the sofa. I picked up the phone and called someone very special.

"Bronnie," I said, giggling, "did you watch me today?"

"Ted," she said, snuffling, "you've had me a nervous wreck all afternoon. I was *so* afraid that Tiger would win, and then you came through. I thought I'd have a heart attack."

"Tiger played good golf. I hit some lucky ones today."

"Yeah," she said. "You were stuck there in the trees. The cameramen couldn't find you."

"But I got the ball where it needed to go."

"And now you're the Canadian Open winner. How

does *that* feel?"

"I'm too full of Canadian Comfort to feel much of anything at the moment," I said. "But I *do* feel tickled by how funny Harold looks right now. He's asleep on the sofa and he's cuddling the trophy."

"Don't you feel larger than life? That you've made history?"

I laughed. "I'm in my mid-thirties and this is my *first* major win. I think a bit of humility and modesty would be in order."

"I have," she said, "some good news, too."

"Let's have it."

"The docs say that there are several cases where the treatment I'm on has been *very* successful. There was this woman in the States? She had what I have, only worse, and the doctors had given up on her, but the radiation did its job and she made a full recovery."

"Sounds encouraging," I said.

"Maybe she's the exception, but it shows that there's still hope for me."

"Well, Bronnie, if a fuck-up like me can win the Canadian Open over Tiger Woods, that tumor in your lung doesn't stand a chance against you."

"Are you in downtown Bayporte?" she asked.

"Yep, still living out of a suitcase. I'd come over at visit you right now, but I'm so drunk that the cops would pull me over. Are you feeling all right?"

"Oh, sure. Looking good, too," she said. "Good color, totally together mentally. My face brightens whenever someone tells me something worth hearing. You know the big problem with illnesses, hospitals and doctors? They're all so *boring*, Ted. I don't get out and exercise. My body still has its lovely suppleness. I'm lonely and horny. It's like I'm stuck here, waiting to die."

"Maybe I *will* drive out there and visit you," I said. "So, your breasts and bum are still as nice as ever, eh?"

"What if they walked in while we were fucking? It would be *so* embarrassing."

"We'd just ask them to leave," I said.

"They probably would, too. They love me around here. They keep shooting me up with morphine because they know it makes me happy."

"Bronnie," I said, "just do me a huge favor. Stay as you are. Great attitude, toughness, resiliency…I don't know how many people I've met who have so many terrific personal attributes."

"Unfortunately," she said, "one of my bad qualities is impatience, and I'm going through an especially horny time right now. So why don't you drink some java, sober up and get on over here one of these days? I think I need the kind of succor you can provide."

As I checked out of the Hotel Bayporte on Monday morning, I couldn't get over the quietude and emptiness of the lobby. Had everyone already forgotten about the Open and its winner? My car sat just outside the front doors, and a pimply kid in a bellman's uniform loaded my suitcases, golf clubs and whatnot into my trunk.

The front desk clerk said nothing about my Canadian Open trophy inches away from her on the counter as she handed me my bill. I signed it just as Harold hurried up to me. He looked as hung over as I felt.

"Where you headed?" I asked him.

"American Midwest," he said. "All kinds of golf